THORNS
by Roscoe G. Beetle

Adult Readers Only

This is a work of fiction. Any names or characters, businesses or places, events or incidents are fictitious and the products of the author's imagination. Any resemblance to actual persons, living or dead, or actual events is purely coincidental.

THORNS

Published by Bewere Books
Flagstaff, Arizona
https://www.bewere.net

ISBN: 978-1-62475-270-4
Printed in the United States, United Kingdom, or Australia
First trade paperback edition: October 2025

Cover art by Hackfurs
Edited by Dirt Coyote and Domus Vocis

This book contains scenes with the following content:

- Domestic Violence
- Drug use
- Dubious Consent
- Homicidal Ideation
- Homophobic Slurs
- Stalking
- Suicidal Ideation

To my wonderful husband; I promise this book is not about us.

FIRST ENCOUNTER:
WAFFLE STATION

MOST of the time, Roy's life was plunged into dark-ness. Companies used to send out their freighters with large crews. In the early days of long-haul space travel, crews could reach up to a half dozen folks maintaining the ship, keeping the freight clean and rotated, and generally keeping one another company. When Roy was younger and got to know the business, he was the low man on the totem pole on a few of those long-haul freights from Venus to just beyond the asteroid belt. Was even happy for a couple years of messing around with the guys, playing cards and catching rats.

Now though, space travel was shrinking. Not in the sense that it was dying off or getting harder, no, but in the sense that the world of a freighter was literally getting smaller and smaller. Gradually, five- or even six-man crews were getting crunched down to three. The newer, sleeker models of ship were automated enough that even that small of a crew had a pretty easy ride through the belt as trips pushed on to Jupiter to mine her moons and harvest gasses from the atmosphere. Three was crunched down to two as smaller and smaller ships were adopted by the freight companies. Finally, two gave way to one.

Roy didn't need to do much – keep his eyes open, keep his paws on the controls, and keep himself from going insane. No more need to kill rats or roaches – all of the cargo holds were vacuum exposed. Great for keeping properly sealed produce, ice, and meat cold with minimal refrigeration. Not so great for any critters who thought they might get a free ride to the next station over with a free meal of vacuum sealed apples. Modern freighters were basically massive cargo holds with engine blocks on one end, and a cab on the front. Where Roy sat, his only companions were a pilot light that flickered no matter how many times he had the bulb changed, a collection of little Pan-Galactic Wrestling tchotchkes he had glued to the dash, and a girly mag he hadn't paid more than a passing glance to in years.

There wasn't much to do, so Roy did whatever he could to stay sane. The cab's controls basically drove themselves – trade routes through the system had been calculated and mapped out by eggheads much smarter than him. Unassisted, he would never be able to find the passage through the meteor swarms that had to be recalculated and navigated yearly to keep the trade passages open. All he needed to do was course correct in case of a DUC, or Direct Unexpected Collision, but they were so rare with all the fancy new sensors and gadgets in these cabs that the number of times he had to take manual control he could count on one hand. Even the horn – a trucker's pride and joy in days of old – had been taken out of his hands by an AI system that automatically hailed ships in his direct route. Computers talking to computers, holding their freighter in open contempt. Roy was sure if it wasn't literally illegal to send unmanned freight out into space, his job would have been toast years ago.

There were dangers, sure. Piracy had never truly gone out of style, but Roy's route was a fairly safe one. He was one of the older freighters still on the payroll – surely coming up on retirement, and The Company knew well enough not to put their older, more vulnerable employees on routes that bordered the lawless frontiers. The old bear was pushing fifty with streaks of grey running inelegantly through his beard. He was fat in the way fat folks who spent most of their life in Zero G were fat – round in the belly and chest, without much in the way of an oblong shape of someone who spent a lot of time in gravity. He exercised of course – that was another way to keep sane on long hauls – but that basically amounted to a resistance bike built into his seat and a couple simulated weight pulls for his arms just to keep them in shape to lift crates once he got to port. His core, already naturally heavy due to his ursine species, was and would always be on the softer side.

So, what does a man do when all he must do for a long trip is eat, exercise, and stare at the same entertainments he brought with him at the beginning of the trip – a trip which has spanned weeks of time not counting rest stops?

In one paw, the magazine sat, hardly open and folded over to one of the more tolerable pictures within – a bovine woman on her knees, arms up and behind her head, and grabbing onto her own short horns. She was thickset in the hips and chest, but not undressed – the model was less dressed in later pages, but Roy never really went that far into the rag anymore. Instead, he held it up in his left paw as a sort of totem – something that represented the act of masturbation, but not something that actively helped in the act. His right paw stroked up and down his cock mechanically. He wasn't hard yet really. He was more bored than horny. His jumpsuit was zipped down below his heavy balls and he had shrugged his way out of his sleeves and pulled up his stained white undershirt. It wasn't particularly comfortable. He couldn't lean back as much as he wanted to, and he had to brace his legs in the exercise bike to steady himself, but he had managed it every other day for weeks. The long, slow stroking of his uninterested cock, until, finally, he would grow erect, relieving the boredom at least for several minutes.

He breathed hard, staring at the displays in front of him. The screens fogged up from his heavy breath as he flicked a thumb over the head of his dick. He gave a little grunt and growled slightly. Frustration mounted. It wasn't working. He wasn't getting hard. He had porn in hand — a hot cow ready for him to stare at and get his rocks off. He wanted to get his rocks off. There was half a day until he would arrive at the next rest stop, and he knew all he would have time for there would be to eat and sleep. This was the only private time he had, and if The Company found out how he was using it, he would get a talking to.

His left arm went limp, resting at his side, as he let his vision go unfocused. He stared through the monitor at the infinite expanse of space outside. Darkness. Nothing and no one around for miles and miles. He was alone. Truly alone. What was wrong? He had forced himself to climax plenty of times doing this.

His eyes darted down, then to the console before him with the array of wrestling action figures he had glued down to the tops. One of the largest, a muscle-bound eagle wearing an anonymizing mask over his face, caught his eye. He stared at the contours of plastic muscles, the tightness of the man's sexless briefs, and the pose, arms up, cocky and self-assured and awkwardly mid flex. Roy's breathing deepened as he felt his loins stir and his paw raced faster, feeling coming over his dick, and finally allowing pleasure to radiate out from his crotch.

His toes flexed in his boots as he stared at the molded

plastic of the wrestler's arm, not even able to unbend itself from the flexed position it was in. His eyes fluttered down to the man's chest and the painted texture of feathers. He gasped, realizing that he was drawing closer to satisfaction.

His eyes darted across the array to another figure, this one shorter and wearing a singlet – a wolf, looking intentionally scrappy and scraggly. A heel, he remembered from his youth following PGW, and one he loved growing up, although he could hardly remember the storylines. However, he recognized that evil smirk on the wolf's face, the shitty way he treated the people around him, talking down to them, berating them. He remembered the sight of the wolf's chest expanding as he stood in the ring, eyes wide, staring hard at his opponent.

"God…" Roy whispered, staring at the plastic toy, and his imagination could finally run wild. He squeezed his cock, hard, and imagined it was the wolf doing the squeezing.

"*Another whore*," he imagined the wolf whispering in his ear, and the imagined words made him shiver, "*Pathetic. Can't even get it up for a woman.*"

He whined, hating himself and loving the apparition riding with him. His body grew warmer, and his strokes grew more desperate. His eyes shot over to yet another figurine of a taller, stockier man. His hero, a puma. He remembered their rivalry. That's right. He nearly heard the announcer on the vid announcing O'neil Lupine and Tex Couger, PGW heavyweight champions, available now on premium stream. A clothesline, and Tex was on the ground. A hold. Lupine was held in Tex's armpit, sweat glistened over their grappling bodies.

He gasped, whining, as the scene played out behind his eyes. That despicable wolf laid out on the mat, legs held wide open by the Puma. Crotch-to-crotch, they rubbed against one another, one struggling and the other reveling in control. Or maybe he preferred the other way, with Tex Couger lying on the ground and the wolf grinding his naked cock against the cleft of his opponent's ass.

He closed his eyes, trying to protect himself from seeing the scene, but unable to escape from it, and unable to stop stroking up and down his cock. His jaw went slack and he moaned, pearls of white shooting from his twitching cock. He gasped and roared before it resolved into a rumbling growl, and then, a small whine as he stared numb at the cum floating towards the ceiling in zero G. He sat for a moment, staring at the blob going by, idly continuing to stroke his meat.

Then, businesslike, he reached into a compartment and pulled out a box of tissues. He caught the floating cum mechanically, soaking it into the tissue, and balled it up two layers deep into a wad before he placed it quickly into the toilet compartment, closed it up, and vented it. There was a harsh suction noise as the toilet vented into a blackwater receptacle on the outside of the cargo hold. Luckily, these tissues were made to be flushed, so The Company wouldn't give him guff for leaving cum stains everywhere again.

He sat for a moment, cock out and rapidly softening as he stared forward, once again looking at his array of wrestlers, now just toys once again. He had done it again. No interest at all in the magazine he had bought, and instead he had imagined...

No. He stopped himself from thinking about it. He tucked his underwear back up, zipped up his jumpsuit, and straightened out his clothing. He reached into a compartment on his side to retrieve a small air freshening spray to try to erase the smell of cum, but that was a losing venture. Freighter cabs were expected to smell after a long voyage. Deodorizing was one of the services the company dock would provide, gratis.

He stuffed the useless magazine back into its compartment and put his paws back on the controls. A few hours to Seb Station. Surely, he could keep his composure until then.

Can't even get it up for a woman.

He furrowed his brow and frowned. Hatred bloomed in his chest, and he chose to pretend that he was angry at the imagined words of O'neil Lupine instead of confronting the truth.

Those were his own words.

Hours later, he pulled into Seb Station. It was the middle of the night – or at least the middle of night in Seb Station's personal time code – and he needed a hot meal and a room and to forget that this ever happened.

Space Station Sebastian was a new stop on Roy's route. The ever-shifting meteor swarm had parted in such a way that his route had to be diverted from his usual stopover in Gerome Station and was likely to be diverted that way for at least the next two or three months. Roy didn't really understand it. He just knew this part of the job was going to be a little different for a little while.

He went through the usual inspections and questions – another reason why at least one person was still needed to drive the cargo – and was clocked out for the day. The Company, of course, provided small cabins next door to the loading docks for their drivers to use, as well as what the old hands called a Triple-S. A tiny cubicle about four by three square with a toilet on one end, a sink on the other, and a showerhead built into the ceiling, getting everything in the room wet. Toothpaste, toilet paper, and other amenities were available in the vending machine down the hall. Not much more room than what is needed to accomplish the three 'S's: shit, shower, and shave. Needless to say, Roy and other freighters like him did not spend much time in their rooms other than to sleep, and usually not even to use the toilet considering twenty-four-hour diners were alive and well on this and countless other rocks throughout the galaxy.

Waffle Station was ancient. Before space travel, before The Company, before extraplanetary wars and space pirates and mercenaries were flying missions between Earth and Mars, Waffle Station existed. It was a humble chain of 24-hour breakfast huts that slowly, steadily, bought out, replaced, and took over nearly every breakfast place in the stations. The accord was clear; you went, you sat, you ordered, you ate, and you got out. Anything more or less than that could earn one the wrath of their employees – who were encouraged to settle up problems with sass and, if necessary, violence – or their fellow customers, who were often tired, frustrated, down-and-out, and forced to eat at the cheapest diner available. The waffles, however, were excellent.

The Waffle Station of Seb Station was busy, as all Waffle Stations were. As Roy walked in, a sour-looking chicken at the counter pointed dispassionately at an empty table nearby. Roy, familiar with the diner's core tenets, sat and picked up the menu for a moment before putting it down again. Bacon, eggs, and a waffle. That's what he always got.

Roy had been through diners like this literally thousands of times. This Waffle Station was no different than any other. It was full of freighters, transients, a few late-night mechanics for the dock, and, at one in the morning local time, drunks stumbling in for a bite to eat. He didn't feel the need to look up. The waiter would come take his order, he would eat, put down his meal card from The Company, and then he would sleep his mandated eight hours. At nine A.M. sharp he would take to the skies again.

The bell over the door rang. A literal bell tied to the front door, and just by chance, Roy glanced up.

The rabbit who walked in the door was shorter than Roy

by quite a bit, although he imagined if those ears that hung back behind his head were held up and erect, they would add quite a bit of height. He stood out because he was wearing a white suit with a red tie, untied around his neck, which set off his black and white fur. He looked around with a grimace at the Waffle Station, and his companion, a lanky-looking donkey who stood at least a foot taller than his companion, immediately broke the mood of the diner with a loud bray. The donkey was wearing a loud, rainbow tee shirt under a black blazer, and was wearing plastic novelty glasses in neon green with the slats going over the eyes.

"God! 'M so *fucking* starving," said the young donkey.

"Mmhmm…" muttered the rabbit, cringing at the younger man's loud, drunken voice.

Roy stared at the rabbit for a moment. It was hard to tell past the snow-white fur and deep black spots, but Roy thought the rabbit looked to be about his age around the eyes and from the lines in his face, although he could tell the guy was making an effort to look younger than that. The rabbit glared up at the harsh fluorescent light, narrowing his eyes at them, and Roy noted that they probably made him look a lot older than he wanted. Before the older rabbit could say anything, the donkey all but pulled him to one side, sitting down at once in a booth across the aisle from Roy's table, giving Roy a full view of them. The rabbit gave Roy a glance, and their eyes met. For a moment there was a look of contrition on the rabbit's face for his guest's behavior, and Roy nodded slowly before the moment was over.

Something made Roy's mouth water, and so he took a sip of the coffee that had been put down in front of him. He didn't ask for it. Everyone got coffee here.

"I havn't been t'one of these since I was a kid," said the donkey, who swayed with obvious drunkenness.

"Yeah," said the rabbit, "Maybe…"

"Huh?"

"Maybe keep the voice…"

"I cn't heeear you, Daddy."

A third voice cut in from somewhere else in the restaurant, "Shut the fuck up!"

The rabbit buried his face in a paw, and with his other he reached over to take the donkey by the arm before he could get up and respond.

"Let's… hey, let's just order, okay?"

The donkey, frowning deeply and bleary eyed, seemed about to pass out any time. He nodded before looking down at the menu.

"Do they have ha'chocklat?"

In a way that sounded almost fatherly, the rabbit rolled his eyes and said, "I'm sure they have hot chocolate."

Still holding the donkey by the arm, Roy's eyes widened as the rabbit, who had to be at least thirty years older than this young donkey, slipped his paw into the donkey's hand intimately. The donkey smiled, forgetting his cares.

"Thanks, Daddy," the donkey said in a loud whisper.

"Yeah," muttered the rabbit, frowning at the pet name.

The sight of this intimate gesture made Roy's eyes go wide. Slowly, Roy looked around and saw several others had noticed this as well. Two men, holding hands intimately, one a lot older than the other. Why had they come in here? They obviously didn't belong here.

The waitress came around and took Roy's order. He kept it short. She then went across the aisle to the rabbit's table, and he, with a charming smile, apologized for his companion and slipped her twenty credits right away. She took it, stuffed it down her bra, and once they'd ordered their waffles and hot chocolate, she wandered away in no hurry.

"Why did you bring me here, kid?" muttered the rabbit.

"I'm hungry an's the only place op'n."

"God you are drunk..."

"Hehe mmhmm... You kept buy'n 'em for me, Daaad-dy..."

"Easy on the cute names here," he muttered, with a glance towards Roy. There was a sudden unsureness in that glance, as if Roy might be dangerous to him. He frowned. "Maybe we should go. Swing by the quikmart on the way to the hotel."

"NO! Come on! I'm starvinggg!"

"Hey, faggot," came yet another voice, and his fur stood on end.

The rabbit went stone stiff, and the donkey, in a sudden, drunken rage, stood up.

"Who the fuck said that?" he demanded.

A fox – another fellow in the company uniform with his jumpsuit stripped down to his waist and tied off to air out his sweat-soaked undershirt – was standing up, a smile curled up his face. Roy stared at him, but the fox didn't even glance his way.

"Nobody wants to see you fairies all over each other. We're trying to eat here."

"Shove off," muttered the rabbit, suddenly all ice. "You don't want to get blood all over your nice company suit. I'm sure you can't afford the fees to get it clean if you're eating in this dump."

"Your blood, maybe. Maybe I'll keep 'em. A little trophy to take with me."

"Y'wanna go?" demanded the donkey, liquor making him bold.

"Sit down Marty."

"M-Morty..." the Donkey said, his brow suddenly furrowed in hurt. "My name is Morti..."

The fox cocked a fist back and punched the young guy, who fell with a cry of surprise and then of pain as his snout smashed into the tile floor. The fox was already laughing as the donkey, suddenly unsure of where he even was, began to crawl away.

"One punch? Really?" the fox said, holding his arms out wide. The rabbit was too busy pushing himself back into the booth to do anything. The rest of the patrons hardly paid attention. "I expected more of a fight from y-"

Roy didn't know what he was doing until the chair was halfway swung. As the fox gloated over his easy victory and the donkey began to cry confused tears with blood streaming down his nose, the bear stood, calmly picked up the sturdy wood and aluminum chair, and swung it hard against the fox's back. The fox, crying out, fell at once to his knees. Roy, idly, thought that the chairs were very well made. It didn't break in his paws as it impacted with the man's back, and when he swung it again, eliciting a second cry from the fox, as well as a whimper, Roy found himself breathing hard.

He turned to look at the rabbit, still cowering, only now from a much larger man wielding a weapon with blood on the edge. The fox was wailing in pain, his arms curling back to press against his injury. The donkey soon wobbled to his feet and ran out of the Waffle Station. However, Roy and the rabbit simply stared at one another, just the edge of fear on his black and white-furred face.

Roy was astonished to see something he had never seen before on the face of anyone, man or woman. Just a flicker of a smile, and a once-over of the man's eyes scanning him from boots to face. He tilted his head, as if considering, but after another moment he let the look drop away.

"Put the fucking chair down!" cried the fry cook behind the counter, an unimpressed looking hound dog with a cigarette hanging out of his mouth.

Hurriedly, as if he had been physically struck by the words, Roy did as he was told, seeming to shrink. Astonishment fell over his own face, eyes wide and a frown forming, and the rabbit, it seemed, was amused. He gave a cold laugh, before he climbed out of the booth, gave the moaning fox a swift stomp on the tail for his own satisfaction, and called out to the fry cook.

"Forget the waffles," he said, "I'm out of here. I need a smoke."

Roy was still standing as he watched the rabbit calmly walk out of the Waffle Station. He stood for a moment, his paws white knuckling the back of the chair as he prepared to sit back down in it. His food would be there soon. He was hungry. He needed to finish his food so he could get to the company apartments and sleep. However, as he watched the form of the rabbit fade into the darkness outside of the plate windows of the diner, he couldn't make himself sit.

He pushed the chair away and followed after, stepping over the still moaning fox. The bell rang as he pulled the door open hard and followed the rabbit into the night, based on... what? A look? A glance? A once-over?

I'm not gay, Roy reminded himself.

The voice of O'neil Lupine he had conjured up hours before, and the excitement he felt as he pursued the rabbit, made him suddenly think twice.

Samuel didn't like to admit it to himself, but he preferred a lot of old things. Cigarette lighters for example. Considering his job, he couldn't smoke much except on excursions like this to the docks, and even then, the younger the people at the bars got, the less sexy they found a gesturing hand with a lit cigarette in it. Only folks in their middle age reliably smoked anymore, but didn't tend to smoke anything with fire, preferring vape pens or just sticking to drinking. The baby gays were all too into clean living.

Thank God for young bucks with daddy issues like... Matthew? Mordechai? Sam didn't remember. The donkey had disappeared into the night by the time he left the Waffle Station, and Sam didn't much feel like tracking him down. The mood was broken, and after he paid for the hotel in advance and everything, all because the kid wanted a meal before they fucked.

He filled his lungs with warm smoke and leaned up against the aluminum-sided wall around the corner from the Waffle Station painted to look like brick. The hotel didn't allow smoking in the rooms either, so this was his only chance to indulge before he headed back. He considered for a while just grabbing a cab back home, but the rideshares were expensive this time of night, and the shuttles during the day were more reliable and, most of all, safer. As if hanging around at the mouth of an alley around the corner from a diner full of space-crazy freighters and desperate transients wasn't dangerous enough.

One ear twitched, always alert. His other ear was half deaf, although he refused to get his hearing checked. Just like he refused to wear his glasses. Just like he didn't like letting kids at the bars see his compression socks, or his knee brace, or the girdle he wore to keep his figure slim. Daddy this, daddy that, but he knew better than to let them see what an actual old fart had to deal with. At least not without attractive mood lighting.

As he took another drag, he was about to stub it out on the wall and move on when a figure came around the corner. A huge figure. A thrill of fear went through Sam's stomach as he clutched onto his cigarette – maybe he could burn out the fucker's eye before he got the shit kicked out of him – but the idea evaporated in a moment. First because the guy was almost too tall for him to reach, and second because he recognized him as that burly bear from the restaurant wearing that company freighter jumpsuit. He relaxed, but only up to a point.

"Well," he said, awkwardly, "Hi."

"H-Hi," the bear said, his back to the streetlamp casting him in shadow.

They stared at one another. Sam was starting to get nervous and reached up to take another shaky puff of his cigarette. The bear simply stood, staring, an imposing shape plugging up the mouth of the alley. He blinked his eyes and turned his head back towards the street, and in the meager light from the streetlamps, it looked as if he was in agony. Good – at least he didn't look angry.

"Having a smoke before I find shelter," muttered Samuel, "in case you were worried I was wandering off into the night."

"That's fine," said the bear.

Sam furrowed his brow, frowning, before he reached down into his pocket and pulled out the pack. Slowly, unsure of what he was doing, he offered the packet to the bear, feeling almost like he was feeding unsafe wildlife as he did.

"Want one?" he asked.

"Okay."

The bear reached forward, took a cigarette and awkwardly began to pat his pockets, miming the act of looking for a cigarette lighter. Sam knew very well he wouldn't have one. From the sweaty, heady aroma Sam could detect, the bear smelled like he was fresh off a long haul, and The Company didn't tolerate anything harder than soda pop in the cab. The rabbit, used to the ritual and thankful for someone to practice it on, dropped his half-smoked cigarette on the ground, ground it out with the toe of his shoe, and pulled out a new one. He put away the pack, brought out his gold-plated lighter, and snapped it open with practiced ease, igniting a small but intense flame to light up his own, before offering it up to the bear. With it hanging from his own mouth, the bear leaned forward, puffing as the flame kissed the tip, casting his face in a red glow, and soon a haze of smoke swirled around the two of them.

Invited in by this ritual, the bear stepped into the alley and leaned up against the wall next to Samuel. He sensed he didn't need to ask. He just did it. He took a lungful of smoke and spoke as he breathed out.

"What happened to your... uh... date?"

"Ran off scared," muttered the rabbit. "Just a kid, honestly. Birthday boy. Just hit twenty-one and his friends had been pouring shots down his gullet all night. I swooped in, put on the charm and..."

"Kinda young."

"Fuck you," Sam said, hardly putting any effort into it. "So... haven't seen you around here before. You must be a displaced freighter from the new route."

"Yup."

"You got a name? Or do I just call you Chair Bear?"

"Roy."

"Roy," Sam repeated, taking another puff. "Sam."

"Sam," Roy repeated.

There was a moment of silence there, and Samuel found himself growing annoyed. He was trying to calm his nerves, and yet here was this guy getting into his space. Sure, he saved Sam from a gay bashing, fine, but what did he *want*? Did he want to know?

"Honestly, I was looking forward to tonight," Sam muttered. "Don't get too many kids too drunk to notice all the... markers of a life well lived. Fucking fox ruining my game."

"You're... gay?"

Sam glanced up at the bear like he was an idiot.

"Did you think we were holding hands because we were best friends?" quipped the rabbit.

"I... I don't..."

"And the fox calling us both fags wasn't a clue? I figured that was why you fucked him up so bad."

"He was bothering you."

"Me? You don't know me," the rabbit muttered. "Why would you do that for me?"

"I... don't know," Roy admitted, fiddling with the cigarette. He wasn't graceful with it like Sam was, holding it between his thumb and forefinger like a joint instead of with the very tips of his fingers. Sam had to admit it suited the strange bear.

"You don't know," muttered Sam, before he smiled. "Well, I've heard stories of serial killers skirting around the law on freighter jobs. Considering how easily you hit that guy, maybe I'm next."

"N-No. I... I'm not..."

"Nah, I know. Just fucking with you," said Sam with a smirk, before he glanced the man up and down. The bear seemed to regard Sam's attention with an odd squirm. Sam smiled. "More likely you've got a pussy in every port just waiting for you. Of course! This is a new stop on the route for you, obviously you're frustrated."

"N-No. I... I don't do that," said Roy, before he gestured towards his heavy face and his unkempt beard. "Too... uh..."

"Ugly?" Sam said, before he shrugged. "Maybe. Not the worst I've seen, and I've been around the block."

"Oh..." muttered Roy, deflating slightly.

Sam smiled. This night was turning around after all. He sensed what Roy wanted – probably even before Roy knew it – and the rabbit was horny and desperate enough to make some bad choices. He sidled closer to Roy then, raising a paw to rest gently against the bear's arm. The bear went tense at the touch but did not pull away. Sam's smile widened.

"Listen, maybe I can pay you back. Y'know, for the help in

there," said Sam, dropping his second cigarette and stamping it out on the ground.

"Uh... Uh-huh?"

"I've got a nice motel room – well, quote-unquote 'nice', but certainly nicer than the shithole The Company's putting you up in. It's all pre-paid, I'm done for the night, and I don't feel like taking a cab home, so... maybe you want to stay for the night."

"S-Stay?"

"Do I need to spell it out?" asked Sam.

With that, the touch became a caress as the rabbit's thinner arm curled around the thick, strong arms of the bear. A small thrill went through the rabbit's stomach. He felt the power in those arms – the power that had knocked that asshole in the Waffle Station down a peg – but the bear was clearly shy and didn't think much of himself. Easy. Probably going to be a lousy lay, but hell, the horny trucker fantasy did appeal, and he already took his pill and had the condoms.

Roy, for his part, simply stared with wide eyes. He blinked, before he nervously puffed his cigarette and, following Sam's lead, dropped it on the ground and stepped on it.

"I never..." he stammered, "with a... I mean, with..."

"A man?"

The bear nodded and Sam's smile took on a kindly smirk as he pushed in closer, leaning his chest against the bear's arm.

"I won't make you do anything weird. A hole's a hole, right? I was ready to take a bigger dick than yours tonight, so..."

"O-oh..." muttered Roy, looking down at his own crotch self-consciously. Sam got another thrill.

"C'mon," said the Rabbit, letting go and stepping out of the alley, "walk me there. I don't relish the thought of running into any more of those mouth breathers from the diner."

Roy, powerless at the orders of this assertive rabbit, said,

"Oh. Okay," and followed obediently.

The Stop-By Motel was just around the corner, and Sam led the gobsmacked bear there. He did not touch him anymore, instead opting to simply look back and smile sometimes. It had been a long time since just a look and a smile was enough, and Sam had to admit he had missed this.

All in all, a microwave burrito, a candy bar, chips, and a tallboy from the Quikmart wasn't actually any more or less healthy than the bacon, eggs, and waffle that he was going to eat at the Waffle Station. Less grease certainly. Not as warm or tasty, but just about as much sugar as would have been in the waffle.

It impressed Roy slightly that Sam had thought of it. This was the only meal he would get for the next leg of the journey, and so Sam waited patiently for him to come out with a plastic bag full of his spoils. Sam was already on his third cigarette when he perked up and smiled that wry smile in Roy's direction, causing the bear to breathe in and out raggedly.

"Finally," muttered the rabbit before he walked on without another word. The Quikmart was next door to the Stop-By Motel, and already the rabbit was digging around looking for his card-key. "You got an early day, yeah?"

"Yes. Nine."

"Day off for me," said Sam, running a paw through the fur on top of his head. "Don't worry. I'll make sure you get where you need to go."

"Th-thank you."

Sam turned to stare strangely at Roy and this sudden deference. He narrowed his eyes and smirked again, and at once, a shiver went up Roy's spine. Out of nerves, he reached into the bag and pulled out the candy bar, unwrapped it, and started to eat. Sam, meanwhile, had turned to walk up the aluminum stairs leading up to the second floor of the motel. His paws were searching his other pocket.

Roy was silent as he walked obediently behind the rabbit. He looked around, taking in their surroundings. This place was low-rent, clearly, set up for transients or backpackers traveling on planetary tours. Each door was set with an electronic lock that took a card key, but heavy granite cinder blocks were set next to each door to act as a doorstop. On top of half of them were ashtrays where half-smoked cigarettes sat stubbed out. Beyond the glass of each window was darkness, covered up by crooked blinds that filtered the artificial moonlight into the room in stark white horizontal bars.

"Shit," whispered Sam, suddenly as he reached the top of the stairs. He reached into his jacket pocket and pulled out his wallet before flipping through a fat stack of cards, growing more and more agitated. He froze, clearly halfway to the room, and furrowed his brow. "Fuck."

"What?" asked Roy.

"I can't find my key," muttered Sam, stashing his wallet away and resuming digging around in his trouser pockets. "Damn it, I thought I…"

"Do… Do we need to go back to the diner?"

"I don't… I thought I put it…?" said Sam, growing visibly agitated, before he sighed, tilting his head back and closing his eyes. "Oh god, no."

"What?"

"Mark had it," said Sam. "I gave it to him when I was flirting."

"You gave him your hotel key?"

Sam turned and snapped at Roy, "Look, it was part of the plan. When we got the key, he wanted to hold it. He was drunk and acting like a child, so I just… fuck. I wanted him to shut up."

"Which door is it? Maybe he's here."

Sam looked around, realizing what Roy meant. If Mark...
Mort? If the kid was drunk and scared, maybe he went to hide
in the hotel room. The night might not be a total bust after all
in that case. Sam furrowed his brow and walked on without
another word to his room: 20C.

The light in the window was on, casting shadows from the
blinds onto the balcony. The door was closed, and when Sam
tried the door, the doorknob simply rattled. Then, the rabbit
stepped up to the window and pressed his nose up to it, shad-
ing the sides of his head with his paws. After a moment, he
yelled loudly.

"Fuck! There he is!" said Sam, furrowing his brow before
he began to beat against the window. "Hey! Kid! Wake up!"

Roy went up to peer into the room as well and found that
through the crooked slats of the blinds, he could indeed see
the donkey, stripped down to his bare chest and underwear,
lying on the bed. His eyes were closed. He was motionless on
top of the covers, dead to the world, and Roy could even see
spots of blood on the pillow where the donkey's bloody nose
had left a stain.

"That asshole locked me out," said Sam, before he redou-
bled his efforts. "Hey! Fucker! Wake up!"

The donkey stirred slowly, obviously so drunk he hardly
knew where he was. With bleary eyes wet and red with tears, he
looked around until his face looked up at the window. His eyes
went narrow. He recognized Sam, clearly.

"Oh, thank God!" muttered Sam, before he smirked and
looked up at Roy. "Maybe the night's turning around for both
of us. You ever spit roasted a drunk frat boy before?"

"N-N..."

"No, of course not," Sam said, his good mood allowing
him to be sultry again, and just a little cruel. "Don't worry, I'll
show you..."

However, before Sam could finish his line, those bars from the light inside disappeared. Sam blinked, turning back to the window. The donkey had turned off the light, rolled over, and gone back to sleep.

"Oh, hell no!" Sam screamed. "That's my fucking room you little cocksucker!"

Roy blinked his eyes before he looked around. He was suddenly aware of where they were. It was the middle of the night on the balcony of a cheap motel. Surely people would be trying to sleep. What if someone came out of their room?

"I'll break this fucking window I swear!" Sam yelled, beating his fist against the glass hard enough to make a sharp rattle, "Open the door right goddamn now!"

This had to stop, Roy knew it. The longer they were here, the more trouble they would be in. Someone was going to come up. What would Roy do? He couldn't get in trouble or else he would lose his job with The Company. He could leave, but Sam's offer loomed large in his mind. He was trapped here on the spot until something gave. If he did nothing, it was going to be bad.

"Hey! Hey, Mario! Open up! Goddamn it, wake the fuck…"

Sam's voice caught in his throat as there was a sudden grunt from next to him. He turned just in time then to see Roy, a boxy object in his arms, just before he leaned back and then pitched it forward into the glass. The granite block sailed from his burly arms, impacted with the glass, and the glass shattered inward, showering the insides. The broken shards cascaded from the windowpane in stages, first the largest shards, shattering loudly against the ground and against each other, then smaller shards, sprinkling over the larger bits with a gentle pitter-patter, and finally a last few isolated splashes of breaking glass. A scream lit up the night from inside as the terrified donkey was awake, aware, and scared out of his mind. All around them, lights in windows lit up.

Sam stared at Roy, whose eyes were wide and wild. His jaw was clenched and he showed sharp teeth. He looked insane, and Sam, not for the first time, worried for his safety. He had gone off with some closet case freak freighter who beat the shit out of a stranger, went to stalk him in an alley, and now broke a window for no reason. This bear was unhinged. Sam felt the urge to run, but strangely, his legs didn't obey him.

"What the fuck is going on up there?" came a voice from down below, and in answer, Sam reached forward and grabbed Roy's massive paw with his own.

"Come on!" he huffed, pulling the bear along to the back staircase of the motel. Already he could hear the sound of whoever was in charge of security rushing up the main stairs. Any minute now they were going to hear sirens. It wasn't a large station, after all. The emergency response could get anywhere within a minute.

The two of them ran down the stairs, Roy trailing behind only slightly. There was nothing at this point keeping them together except their shared crime, and the fact that they were paw in paw as they ran down the alley behind the motel, circled around, and began to make their way towards the docks.

The door to Roy's apartment opened, and Sam stood, staring at the blank white walls. It was two-thirty in the morning at this point. They had been out on the street avoiding sirens for several minutes. They had shared the microwave burrito, cold, and had been passing the tallboy between one another to calm their nerves, and, finally, without anyone needing to ask permission, Sam had come with Roy to his company room.

"Tiny," muttered Sam as he walked in, followed closely by Roy. "How do you even sleep in a space like this?"

"The cab is smaller," muttered Roy, closing the door behind him. "You want to use the shower, or…?"

"I'll shower in the morning," muttered the rabbit, before he turned to stare at the single cot, hardly big enough for Roy to sleep on. "Is that…?"

"You can take the bed. I'll, uh…"

"Sleep on the floor?" said Sam, doubtful that was even possible. There was, if possible, even less floor space than there was space on the bed. "I guess the mood was shattered a bit."

Sam sat down, stretching his arms, before he started to take off his jacket and unbuttoned his shirt. Roy stared at him as he did, and the rabbit's fingers slowed to a crawl.

"I… er…" muttered Roy, aware that he was making things awkward, "sorry."

"What were you thinking, throwing a brick through the goddamn window?"

"I… I was just… he wasn't waking up. I thought… you said…"

"You thought breaking a window would help, huh?" scolded Sam, "They're going to charge that window to my card, y'know? I'm probably out a hundred creds because of you."

"Oh."

"Unless you pay."

"I… I can. I have money saved up. I'll pay you back."

Sam narrowed his eyes and scowled. What was with this guy? Slowly, Sam smirked anew and shrugged, before he continued to unbutton his shirt.

"Well, that'll be just fine. Not like this night could get any worse."

"You want to sleep," said Roy, staring at the floor. "I'll, er, I'll shower and…"

"Wait," muttered Sam.

Roy looked up and met Sam's eyes, and the rabbit stared right back. After a moment, the rabbit scooted to one side and patted the side of the bed. Idly, he tugged at the collar of his half-buttoned shirt, and a gray patterned fuzz sat exposed over his flat, lanky chest. Roy's eyes drifted from the man's eyes to his chest.

"Sit," ordered the rabbit.

Obediently, Roy sat next to the rabbit on the side of the bed. He had been nothing but a nuisance today. He wanted to do whatever was necessary for Sam to get him through this night. It was the least he could do.

Roy's racing thoughts were suddenly interrupted by a hand on his chest. His heart immediately began to race as Sam laid a paw over his thick, soft pecs, brushed his nipples through the thick material of his jumpsuit, and, with clever fingers, found the zipper and began to pull it down.

"What are you...?"

"Before you shower," muttered Sam. "You've been in a cab for how long now?"

"Each leg is about two days."

"Heh," muttered the rabbit, before he leaned towards Roy, pulling open the front of his jumpsuit and hovering his nose inside. Roy stared, eyes wide, as the rabbit took a heavy sniff of his body, and he saw the rabbit's nose twitch and his long ears shudder. "Whoof..."

"Is it... bad?"

"Objectively speaking, yes," said the rabbit, sounding as if he had been running a marathon suddenly, "but it's been a long time since I had someone who didn't smell so pretty."

"I thought... I thought you wouldn't want to...?"

In answer, Sam unzipped the front of the jumpsuit further with a smirk.

"I've been cockblocked, had to run around the streets at night, and all I had to eat is half a burrito, some beer, and far too many birthday cake shots. If I don't get something out of tonight, there is no justice in the world."

Roy gasped as the rabbit's paw snaked down the front of his jumpsuit and grabbed his cock through his underwear. Sam's eyes widened, and he nodded, seeming impressed enough.

"Shower later," whispered Sam. "Strip."

The order was obeyed promptly as Roy finished unzipping his jumpsuit and stood to let it fall all the way to the ground, leaving him in his sweat-stained undershirt and boxers. He kicked off his boots and socks, and stepped out of his clothes, before he reached up to take off his shirt.

"No, leave that on," said Sam, who was slowly stripping himself to match as he leaned against the bare wall of the tiny apartment. "Makes you look like trash."

Roy felt a pang of shame at that comment, but he obeyed. Something about Sam's tone — as if he was degrading himself by sleeping with Roy — was getting Roy excited. He didn't know what he was doing, or how to do it, but he wanted it. He wanted it bad. A tent formed in his boxers and Sam smiled at it.

He reached forward and touched Roy's thick tool, and Roy gasped at the feeling. The sudden spike of pleasure took him off guard. There was no awkward foreplay with any magazines needed here. No desperate daydream. Sam's paws were around his hard cock, and they were so fucking soft.

Sam pulled his underwear down, yanking the cock into view. Once again, Sam smelled it, his nose wrinkling at the sharp odor, but it made him just smile more.

Out of the jacket that was now on the floor, Sam pulled a little bottle out, as well as a roll of condoms. Then, with his other hand, he pushed Roy back to sit on the bed and to lean up against the hard wall.

"We're going to make this quick," hissed Sam in Roy's ear.

"Okay."

Soon, the rabbit was straddling his hips and he felt a sudden warmth. Sometime during all of that, Sam had taken off his trousers and briefs, and sat in Roy's lap, rubbing his length against Roy's. Neither of them were huge, but the fact that Roy was bigger and taller made his own cock look smaller in comparison. Sam's dominant attitude was making that even more clear.

"Pathetic," whispered the rabbit in the bear's ears, sensing that the bear would like that. "This better be worth my time."

"Y-Yes…"

"Yes, what?"

Roy thought for a moment, before he gave a small rumbling mumble and muttered, "Y-Yes… sir?"

"Better," said Sam before he rewarded the bear with a hard grip of his erection. Roy gasped at the mix of pain and pleasure. Roy looked down and watched as Sam tore the condom package with his mouth, pulled it out, and rolled it down the big bear's cock.

"A-Ah!" said Roy at the unfamiliar feeling of latex against his cock.

"Heh. So, am I your first? Or am I just your first man?"

"I've… I've been with…"

"Oh? Trying to prove something with some piece of ass?" hissed Sam, sensual and cruel in equal measure as Roy felt his paw stroke up and down his cock, spreading an oily lube over it. "Maybe trying to stop people from thinking you're a fag?"

"M-Maybe…?"

"And yet, here we are," whispered Sam, spreading his legs and hovering his ass over the bear's cock. "It didn't work, did it? Hell, you're so hungry for me, I bet I could bend you over the bed and fuck you myself. I bet you'd beg if I wanted you to."

"P-Please…"

Sam looked down. The tip of Roy's cock was kissing his

loose entrance.

"Filthy trucker," whispered Roy. "If you want it, say 'thank you, Samuel, Sir.'"

"Th-Thank... thank you, Samuel, Sir. May I...?"

Roy reached up with his paws to encircle Sam's hips. It gave Sam pause how the man's big paws fit almost completely around his thin frame. Roy was a big man, deceptively strong, and violent too. The thought of it, that this man was unhinged and violent, and yet, was here begging to fuck him, sent a fresh shot of pleasure through Sam's loins. Who needs pills when you have a shot of adrenaline like this? Nevermind that Sam had taken his little blue pill discreetly as he left the bar and probably only had a couple hours to take advantage of it.

If Roy wanted to, he could kill Sam dead right now. It wouldn't even be hard.

Instead, Sam grabbed hold of those paws and then began to lower himself down, pressing his ass against Roy's thick cock. He gasped, throwing his head back at the pain of his entrance stretching – beautiful pain that would lead to something more. Roy's eyes went wide as his mouth fell open. Sam saw the man's sharp teeth and lolling tongue, and the rabbit reached up to put his thumb in the bear's mouth. In surprise, Roy closed his lips and began to lick and suck around the rabbit's thumb, unsure of what Sam wanted from him as he lowered himself down onto Roy's cock.

Roy couldn't hold back. He bucked up, trying to sink himself into the rabbit's hole faster, and Sam gasped and tightened the pressure of his thumb on the bear's tongue.

"Slow," he demanded.

Roy did not nod, but he did stop moving his hips, or at least tried. He was quivering from the tight pressure around his dick as Sam sank deeper and deeper, taking in more of his cock. Sam's face scrunched up in concentration as he breathed

heavily, getting used to the bear's tool, and the look on the rabbit's face was intoxicating. Roy was doing this. Every pant and
shudder; he was causing it.

Soon, Sam's ass met Roy's crotch. He was fully hilted, and
he felt the rabbit's hard cock throbbing against his soft belly. Despite the look of dreamy, bleary concentration on Sam's
face, he forced himself to smile and pressed down once again
on the bear's tongue.

"Fuck me."

Roy's movements were clumsy, desperate, and all in all
Sam grimaced at the graceless way he drove his cock into the
rabbit's hole. Even so, it was a familiar feeling. His dick was
good enough to get in; to rub against his walls. It wasn't good.
It wasn't comfortable. Roy didn't take care with the body he
was using. He was rutting hard into the rabbit, racing to climax.
Sam's self-assured smile faded at the feeling of the bear using
his body, and he felt the power gradually shift. He was on top,
still, but Roy, suddenly, was in control.

The bear reached up with one arm to wrap around the
rabbit's midsection as he bucked his hips up, and Sam couldn't
tell him off between the gasps that the bear elicited from him.
Roy, for his part, was silent except for a few growls and gasps,
as if he was deep in a trance. Sam's legs were growing tired.
The brace was helping but his knees were wearing out, and the
bear's lack of support or care for him was making the whole
experience difficult.

"F-Fuck..." Sam managed to say, "G-God, slow... slo...
slow d-down..."

Roy did not slow down. Something had tripped inside of
him, something primal. Something Roy had never tapped into
before. Sam's nose was buried suddenly in Roy's neck. The rabbit realized that the sweaty stench of the bear was surrounding
him as surely as the bear's arms. Suddenly, Sam cried out as

he felt gravity upend itself, and he was falling backwards. Roy had swung him around, laying him down on the bed, pressing him down with his fat body, and thrust harder now that he had more leverage. Sam was powerless to stop it. The fat bear's limbs were stronger than they looked. He remembered how easily the bear had picked up that granite block and how hard he had swung that chair. The thought of the bear doing such casual violence made Sam frightened, and, despite the discomfort, and the over-eager drilling fucks, and the weird wordless grunting, Sam found himself growing harder. His dick rubbed up against the bear's thick belly, and he reached over the side of the bed to brace himself against the bottom of the squeaking bed frame.

"A-ah…" Roy began grunting. "Ah!"

It was a throaty moan, harshly bellowing in Sam's ear. He felt the man getting close, and he realized what was about to happen. The heavy body was pressing down against his chest. He couldn't breathe or talk, nor did he want to, and consequently he felt himself going limp as the bear used his body for his own satisfaction.

Sam's own climax took him completely by surprise. He didn't realize how close he really was. He cried out, hardly able to make a sound as he lay underneath the heavy body of the bear, but he felt his own hips begin to buck as wet cum began to erupt across their bellies. He choked out a gasp, wanting to scream and cry – half in pain and fear at being suffocated, and half in pleasure and to beg the bear not to stop. Eventually, however, the bear, too, began to erupt, his own voice crying out in surprise, voice growing higher pitched and uncharacteristically effeminate as Sam's ass milked his cock.

He continued to thrust for several seconds, chasing that dreamy, empty high for as long as possible and grinding the rabbit into the mattress so hard that Sam began to grow panicky. He couldn't breathe. Pins and needles started to work their way down his legs, and his chest began to burn. There was suddenly life in his limbs, and he quickly began to slap the bear's sides. Roy, slowly, lifted himself up, and Sam managed to breathe in painfully. His ribs felt bruised, and as he took in a breath, he felt suddenly light-headed, and hyperventilated for a moment before he reached forward to grab hold of the bear's large belly, ironically seeking comfort from the very thing that had nearly killed him.

"You... fucking... idiot..." muttered Sam, blearily. "You could have killed me."

Despite his words, he was pressing himself against the larger man's body, and Roy was sitting back on his haunches. Slowly, they were switching places, Roy lying back on the bed as he grappled with what he had just done to the other man, and Sam leaning towards him to press himself against the comforting softness of the bear's body.

"Fffffffuck," said Sam as he realized that he was still cumming a little, staining the bear's fur in his essence. He looked down at the large load trapped inside the tip of the bear's condom. It hadn't been the best sex he ever had. Hell, it was kind of awful. But still, Sam couldn't stop himself from leaning forward until finally, they had inverted completely, with Roy lying back fully and Sam using the bear's body as a massive pillow.

"Whew... alright," muttered Sam, "I could use a smoke right now. Don't suppose they allow smoking...?"

"No."

"Damn," he muttered.

"Did I...? Was...? Was I good...?" stammered Roy, obviously still coming down from the high of claiming Sam's ass as his own. Sam paused for a moment.

"Not really," he said, truthfully. "You got the spirit though. I bet you could figure it out."

"Sam…" said the bear, raising his paws to encircle the rabbit.

The rabbit allowed it because there really wasn't anywhere else to go. No matter what, he was going to stay the night here. Might as well enjoy it.

"I… I love you."

Sam's eyes widened and he stared at the bear for a moment, before he snorted in laughter. He looked at the bear like he was an idiot, and at once, Roy shrank back, frowning.

"No, you don't," muttered Sam, "Go to sleep."

With that, Sam said nothing else. He simply closed his eyes. Roy, with the body of the rabbit on top of him, could hardly sleep. He had slept with someone. He had done things he had only imagined doing with another person, let alone with a man. He felt his hands run up and down the rabbit's soft fur and dreaded the morning.

SECOND ENCOUNTER:
RIFF-RAFF

ROY was squirming as he pulled into Seb Station. It had begun a month before, as he was spending his usual rest period on DSR-03 waystation just outside the asteroid belt, when he was informed that the change to his new route would persist beyond the short time his dispatchers said. It seemed a DUC in the asteroid belt had turned the whole zone into a billiards table a little before his last haul two months prior, and that was why the route had changed so suddenly. Eventually it would settle, he knew. His old route was well-established, and much shorter than the current way that went through Sebastian. The Company would be working to clear the route enough to send freight through the proper way again, but The Company worked slow and cheap. Inevitably he would have to go through Seb many more times before he was put back on his normal route.

The memory of Sam haunted Roy. He wasn't even sure Sam would be on Seb still. That was two months ago after all. People did live on Sebastian – it was a populous space station due to its orbit around Jupiter and people lived there on lunar mining claims and The Company's sponsorship. Roy had rarely gone out of his way to visit anywhere on any station but the dockside wards. He was a Mars planetsider and became a freighter as a young man, and while he technically still had residence back home, he spent only a couple months in his apartment every year or so on his off-times. He didn't know for sure whether Sam lived on Seb, if he had been a transient worker, or something else.

The memory of the soft feel of that black and white fur with the little shock of grey among his chest made Roy squirm as he walked from the docks to the Waffle Station. It was, once again, one in the morning. Food. Rest. That's all he needed. Wondering and chasing after that rabbit would be useless. Food. Rest. Roy walked along the streets of Seb Station, hands in his pockets. He felt himself through the pockets of his jumpsuit. He was getting hard already. Scenes were playing through his head, the same way they played through his head every day of the last two months crammed inside that cab, until he had nearly run out of tissues. He knew he would get a talking to when they found the blackwater basin crammed full of twice as much paper as anything else.

Food. Rest. He saw the neon sign of the Waffle Station. Nothing like that would ever happen to him again. He was sure of it. Sam told him as much. He wasn't good enough. He was fat, ugly, and violent. He had cost Sam a hundred credits and had to pay him back in the morning for that broken window. They'd said nothing at all about sex or seeing one another again. They didn't exchange numbers. Sam just demanded his money, lit up a cigarette, and the two of them parted.

He walked towards the door, ready to push his way inside. He hoped they didn't remember him from two months ago. He didn't want anyone to recognize him here. He would eat, immediately go back to the company apartment with the triple-S, go to sleep, and leave. Until then he could not relax.

However, the smell caught him before his paw could touch the push-bar on the door. Cigarette smoke. The smoke entered his nose and shot straight through his body, making him stand up straight. It was as if electricity had gone up his spine, starting from the base of his tail and ending just behind his eyes. He blinked and sniffed, and his eyes widened. Finally, filled with equal parts dread and elation, he turned to look.

There he was, leaning against the plate glass window of the Waffle Station. Unlike the stylish suit and tie he had been wearing two months prior, Sam instead wore a casual blazer over a turtleneck sweater. He had on black leather gloves, and the white stub of a cigarette popped against them. His legs were skinny, stuffed into tight jeans, and he wore brown dress shoes with no visible socks. The flash of the man's ankles, one shock white and one shiny black, made Roy's mouth water.

"Hey," said the rabbit after a moment while the bear stared hard. "C'mon."

Without another word, Sam turned and started to walk away, dropping the stub of his cigarette on the curb, stomping it out, and walking on in the same smooth movement. Roy watched that maneuver with fascination. Was this even real?

"You coming?" demanded Sam, turning back and starting into his eyes with annoyance.

"Oh..." said Roy, rushing after him, "S-Sam..."

"Roy, right?" asked the rabbit, eyes half-lidded as he stuffed his own hands in his pockets.

"Yes," he answered. "I thought... Why...? I need to eat and..."

"What? You'd rather eat diner food? I know a better place," he said, and somehow Roy knew there was to be no more argument. "Dive bar, but kitchen stays open late, plus we can get a drink."

"I thought... I mean... after last time..."

Sam merely shrugged, "Don't get full of yourself. I happened to be free tonight, and I figured with your route switched over for the next God knows how long, you'd need to unwind. So do I. Been a hell of a month trying to sort out that nightmare."

"You... work for The Company?"

Sam smirked, then looked up at the other man. A dangerous-looking smile, Roy thought, but that wasn't a problem. Sam couldn't be half as dangerous as Roy was.

"Not directly. Import-export," said Sam, "Fantastic money, but requires me to live in the ass end of nowhere, which suits me fine. Gets me away from my fucking ex, so *c'est la* fucking *vie.*"

"Your ex... husband?"

"Wife," Sam corrected him, with a sudden frown. "No more about that. Better left in the dust at this point. We're here."

Roy looked up. Another neon sign greeted him in alternating red and purple, which declared this bar to be called 'Riff-Raff.' Of course, Roy looked past the sign. It hardly seemed to be a place of business at all, let alone a bar. It was instead an otherwise nondescript door in an aluminum wall of one of those boxy units where he figured that seasonal workers and mining families lived. He felt anxious suddenly. What was he doing here? He just followed the rabbit without thinking.

Sam opened the door without a fuss and lazily held it open for the bear, and Roy hesitated for only a moment before he stepped forward. The door opened onto a staircase leading down, and as soon as the door opened, he heard muffled drums of some kind of hard music. Sam led him down the stairs towards another inner door at the bottom, and there he opened a plain-looking basement door.

Immediately, noise hit Roy. A hard rock song played over the sound system, but no one was dancing. The few people there were seated at the bar – most in tee-shirts and jeans or in jumpsuits very much like Roy's – and were nursing beers while looking bleary-eyed. No one was together here. All were separated, except for Roy and Sam, who walked in together. The lights were strangely bright, like the rec room basement at a friend's house Roy remembered playing in as a kid, and there was even a pool table over in the corner to complete the illusion.

"What it lacks in ambiance, it more than makes up for in discretion," said Sam, sensing Roy's confusion at these surroundings. He turned to the bartender and barked out, "Vodka soda, and…?"

He stared at Roy expectantly, and the bear only hesitated for a moment before he said, "B-Beer. Whatever's cheap."

"Well, cheap date," said Sam with a lilt, in that tone that made Roy's fur stand on end. *You look like trash.*

The bartender hardly looked up as he did a messy, generous pour of cheap-looking well vodka with a spritz of soda. Then he picked up a brown bottle, popped the cap, and slammed it down hard enough that it began to fizz. They each took their drink and walked across the shag carpet to a corner table. The beer was overflowing and started to drip down across the bear's paw. He was afraid for a moment the bartender would tell him to get a napkin or something, but the drops landed on the carpet below, and it was clear to Roy the carpet had seen worse days.

Sam sat. Roy sat beside him. They each took a sip of their drinks.

"So," said Sam, with a grimace at the strong drink, "Freighter, huh?"

"Yes."

"Crunched up in that tin can all month," said the rabbit, not looking at Roy, and instead glancing up at a muted television that was playing a late night rerun of some slickly produced dreck from a decade ago. "What's that like?"

Roy paused, staring at the rabbit. He breathed in, out, took another drink, and then managed to force himself to speak. "Fine."

"Fine...? Really? Sounds hellish. You're an old hand at it too. They don't hire new freighters older than maybe thirty."

"Started when I was nineteen," Roy said, quietly. "Straight out of high school."

"Forty-eight?" guessed Sam.

"F-Forty-five," muttered Roy.

"Whoops."

Roy shrugged and took another drink. He looked at the rabbit, narrowing his eyes, and tried to guess as well, "Forty... Seven?"

"Hah! I wish," muttered Sam, before he glossed over the actual answer and continued to ask Roy another question, "Why, though?"

"Wh-Why? Why what?"

"Why'd you leave home at nineteen? Why leave home for half a year hauling freight in the middle of nowhere?"

The bear frowned, furrowing his brow before he answered, "I don't know. It was something to do. Wasn't so bad at first."

"Yeah, I've seen the deathtraps they have you riding in now, sheesh," muttered Sam. "I bet if you died in there nobody would find the body until you pulled into the next station."

"Happened once," Roy muttered, "Friend of mine. Used to haul in his crew back when the ships were bigger. Older'n me. Heart attack en route, and nobody knew until they opened the cab's airlock."

"Shit," muttered Sam, turning to stare at Roy. Roy realized

the horror on the rabbit's face.

"Sorry."

"W-Whatever," the rabbit said, before he shrugged, "I guess I was the one who stepped in it."

"Why do you want to know so much about me?" asked Roy, suddenly, eyes widening, "Why did you... why did you bring me here?"

Sam stared for a moment, thinking of what to say, before he smirked once again and took a sip of his vodka. Then, he finally said, "The trucker thing. It's pretty hot, y'know?"

"That's it?"

"I mean, last time? It wasn't *so* bad," muttered Sam, "I mean, it *was*. I got fined more than the hundred creds you gave me you know."

"Oh... I can... I can pay the difference..."

"Forget about it!" snapped Sam, "Let's just say... the idea of somebody getting up and leaving their life behind for half a year sounds... kinda... I dunno..."

"It isn't," Roy said, his voice low and his tone dark, "It's lonely. Used to be someone there to talk to. Not anymore. Just you alone in a cabin for days and days and days."

"Maybe that's it, then," Sam said, seeming desperate to try to justify this meeting to himself as well as to Roy. "Someone to talk to."

"You have people."

"One night stands hardly count and get fewer and further between as time goes by, and it's not like I have too many people to talk to in the office."

"Import-export," muttered Roy. "What's that like?"

Sam shrugged, "Better than a sharp stick in the eye."

An evasive answer. Sam clearly didn't want to talk about himself, Roy knew. He took another drink of his vodka soda and it was as if Roy had never asked anything at all.

"What do you, er, do in a cabin alone for all that time, anyway?"

"Think," muttered Roy, staring at Sam. "I've been thinking about you."

"I'm sure you have," muttered the rabbit, refusing to meet the bear's gaze, "and what about..."

However, Roy wasn't done, "I've been thinking about you. About your... cigarettes, and that kid screaming in the hotel room, and the... the things you said to me. I never thought I'd see you again. I thought you hated me."

"Hate is a strong word," muttered Sam. "I hardly know you."

"Why *do* you want to know me?" asked Roy, "You've been asking me questions all night."

"Just... curious."

"And you haven't answered any of mine. Not really."

"Well, that's none of your goddamn business, is it?" Sam retorted, scowling up at the bear. "You don't have to answer me if you don't want to."

"I... I want to, though. I... I'd like to know you," said Roy, slowly raising his arm to touch the rabbit... somewhere. Anywhere. He hesitated, trying to decide whether to wrap it around his shoulder, around his waist, or to rest it on his leg, or to perhaps take his paw in his own. However, before he could, Sam leaned away from him.

"Don't get the wrong idea here, Roy," said Sam, harshly. "I'm not here because I'm interested in anything deeper than another fuck, understood? I'm not your boyfriend. You don't love me. Understood?"

"Y-Yeah."

Sam stared at the bear as he turned away, staring up at the TV where a long infomercial for a gimmicky cleaning product was playing out. A bright-eyed little twink was fluffing up the latest and greatest innovation in kitchen sponges, and by the time Sam followed the bear's gaze up to the screen, the commercial was done and a black and white scene of a housewife struggling to stack plastic tubs in her cabinets began to play.

"I haven't had anything like... like you happen to me since I was a kid," muttered Roy then, as they both solemnly watched TV as they nursed their drinks.

"Not with a man, I presume. I seemed to be under the impression I was your first."

"A woman," Roy said, "I barely knew her. I... She was a girl in high school with me. I... I thought I'd try... and..."

"Didn't like it?"

Roy shook his head before he said, "I did it anyway."

Sam stared at the bear. Then, forgetting the TV, he slammed his drink down on the table, deep in thought. He grumbled slightly before he shrugged his shoulders and said, "Yeah. I think I get it. Hard not to catch feelings when it's basically your first time. I remember being there."

"Oh."

"I was way, *way*, too young when I married my ex," he said, leaning his face against his paw with his elbow rested against the table, lost in the unpleasant memory. "Straight out of college. Fuck. She never stopped resenting me for 'ruining her career' when I knocked her up. She could not wait to get away from me once the nest was empty."

"You have a kid?"

"Two. Boys," Sam muttered, before he furrowed his brow and harshly recited, "Anyway, a hole's a hole, so it was never about me fucking the pool boy or whatever. Maybe I fucked around a little, maybe she did too, maybe it just wasn't meant to be. The money was the worst part. Took me years to recover. Had to move all the way out to bumfuck nowhere wheeling and dealing import taxes and tariffs to make ends meet and get as far away from the family as possible. There. I talked about myself. Happy?"

"Two boys," muttered Roy, blinking his eyes. "Have you seen them...?"

"Recently? Not really. I keep in touch with my eldest, but the younger one hates my fucking guts just like that bitch does."

Sam was getting worked up, clearly, and so Roy sensed it was time to change the subject. He picked up his beer, took a swig, and found that he had emptied it.

"Beer's done," he muttered. "I need to eat something before bed."

"I'll get us some fries and a sandwich," said Sam, standing up. "Another round too. I'm feeling generous. After I take a piss, of course. I'll put in the order and... er..."

Sam looked at Roy then, strangely, almost as if he was considering something. He frowned, before he turned and walked back up to the bar. He said a few words to the bartender, who merely glanced up and then back down, before Sam started to walk towards the back of the bar where the bear could see a sign above an alcove with a picture of a toilet on it.

However, before Sam disappeared into the alcove, he turned. Once again, he hit Roy with that look, considering his move, and Roy simply stared from his seat in the corner. Slowly, a smile crept up the side of Sam's face, and, almost imperceptibly, the rabbit tilted his head towards the alcove.

Roy's eyes went wide as Sam soon disappeared around the corner. Was the rabbit suggesting what he thought he was suggesting? The bear was paralyzed for a moment by indecision until the bartender disappeared from his post to deliver their order to the kitchen. Roy took that as his signal, and he stood to follow the rabbit into the bathroom.

Warm wetness engulfed Roy's cock as the rabbit's velvety

mouth slowly sank down to the root. Roy leaned up against the toilet basin, sitting heavily on the closed seat, and whimpered, biting the side of his hand to keep himself from crying out. Images ran through his mind. Scenes, pornos he'd forced himself to sit through, of women giving head to men muttering stilted, unenthusiastic filth. The memory of that girl— what even was her name? When she tried to put her muzzle around him, choked, and gave up, focusing instead on letting Roy climb on top of her.

This wasn't like either of those extremes. It wasn't like porn – somehow sterile and fake, with a camera constantly demanding you pay attention to whatever body part you were supposed to be interested in – and it wasn't like an inexperienced blowjob from a teen girl who barely wanted to fuck you. Roy had only known professional discipline or mild disgust before. To see someone so eager to go down on someone else would have been unthinkable, and yet as Roy stared down at the top of Sam's head, it seemed like he was in another world.

His eyes were closed as his head bobbed up and down Roy's cock, the tongue and the back of his throat teasing the head and sliding up and down the shaft. With his soft paws, he fondled the bear's thick balls. Roy's big belly hid most of the actual action from him, as he never quite got to see the tip of his cock enter Sam's mouth, and Sam hadn't been altogether interested in foreplay before this. Roy felt almost like he was a voyeur to the act; that he was watching from outside of his body as Sam sucked some other man's dick. The thought almost made him more excited, and his breathing hitched.

He felt himself getting close. His breathing changed. He gasped as that sweet wetness engulfed him once again down to the root, and the light suction made him whimper.

Then, a sudden shock. He felt a slap on his thigh and his eyes went wide as Sam delivered a sharp, soft smack. That was the first time Sam looked up and met Roy's gaze with his own. Just over the mound of his belly, those narrow eyes seemed pleased by the mess he was making of Roy's composure.

"S-Sam..." whined Roy, warmth was spreading. His hips were beginning to move slightly, sitting up from the toilet he was seated on. He felt his cock throb – he felt it! It hardened. He was so close. He couldn't believe it. He gasped again, trying to say Sam's name.

Then, he felt a pinch at the base of his cock and that hot wetness left him. Sam took a deep breath as he pulled his mouth off the bear and stretched his jaw. He resolved into a slight smirk as Roy squirmed, desperate to cum, right on the edge, but unable.

"God you're like a fucking teenager," whispered Sam, aware that they were in a public bathroom after all. He took a moment to peer towards the stalls on either side, making sure no one had come into the room. "Calm down. Think about... baseball or something."

"B-Baseball...?"

"I dunno. I read that once," Sam said, standing up. His knees popped and the rabbit gave a slight groan as he let go of Roy's cock and then leaned up against the larger man, reaching up to fondle the man's chest. Another smirk. "We got all night, don't we?"

"I... need... need to sleep. Last time I..."

"Last time we were doing it in a fucking cubicle," Sam hissed, bitterly. "This time I got us a room. No broken windows this time please?"

"You... You got...?" muttered Roy, leaning back. "When did you get a room?"

"Before I picked you up," said Sam, shrugging as he casually rested his chin on Roy's chest, smelling the sweat coming from his undershirt.

Indignation rose up in Roy's chest. He furrowed his brow and asked, "What if... What if I didn't...?"

"Oh, you would, I knew," Sam taunted, tilting his head and looking at Roy like he was an idiot, "pathetic little closet case. Where else would *you* get a piece of ass this fine?"

Roy felt his breath quicken again. Shame. And yet, he felt himself get harder. His cock jumped, and Sam felt it against his leg and let his smile widen. Roy could see the man's buck teeth suddenly. He was normally more reserved with his smiles – all smirks and glances and demure little grins – but now he couldn't help himself. Roy knew Sam was getting off on jerking him around. He should have pushed the man off him, zipped up his jumpsuit, and ran out, but something made him lean back, pressing his back against the toilet basin as he surrendered to that buck-toothed smile. His heart beat faster. He longed for Sam to kneel back down, or for them to skip the meal and head straight for the motel, but instead, Sam just reached down and took Roy's shaft in hand.

"Here's how tonight is going to go, Roy," whispered the rabbit. "We're going to go back out there, eat, and then go straight to the motel – but we are going at my pace tonight, understand?"

"Y-Yes..."

"When I say slow down, you say...?"

He felt the paw tighten around his cock, just on the edge of pain.

"Y-Yes, sir."

"Good," said Sam, letting go of him. Roy was almost sorry about that.

"Are... Are you...?" said Roy, eyes widening, a sudden fear inside him, "are you going to... f-fuck me?"

Sam blinked his eyes before he laughed, pressing his face against the bear's belly as he did.

"You ever bottomed before, Roy?"

"N-No…?"

"Then no, I'm not fucking you tonight. Probably a disaster area down there," muttered the rabbit, before he shrugged and caressed the man's round gut. "Maybe we'll work up to it for another time."

"Another…?" muttered Roy, "You want to…?"

Sam frowned, realizing he'd caught himself making plans. He cleared his throat and pulled his affectionate paws away from Roy. He stood up fully, minimizing contact between the two of them – even though they were both stuffed inside this toilet stall and their legs at least had nowhere to go but to press together with Sam standing up between Roy's.

"Don't," said Sam, "Don't make it anything more than what it is."

"What… What is it?" asked Roy, and the sheer confusion and distress in his voice was not lost on the rabbit.

"Just sex, alright?" Sam growled.

Both men jumped when they heard a sudden knock on the stall door. Sam turned around fully, startled, and in a moment of weakness leaned back against Roy's body. By reflex, Roy reached up and wrapped an arm protectively around the rabbit while his other arm pressed against the stall wall. Were they caught? Were they in trouble? Roy's eyes widened and all thoughts of sex left him. Someone was standing on the other side of the stall door. Roy looked down and saw beat up sneakers.

"Fucking quit it," came the nonplussed voice of the bartender. "Food's ready."

And then the sneakers turned away and were gone.

Sam and Roy stayed like that, entangled in the bathroom for another moment, before Sam forced a laugh and once again stood up. He looked down to see if he could play with his prey a little more, but found that Roy's cock had softened from the stress and was hanging limp. Sam sighed, unlatched the door, and stepped out, not even bothering to give Roy a chance to zip up.

"Get dressed," said Sam, and soon he left the bathroom.

Roy sat, the stall door hanging open, as he was suddenly alone in the bathroom. Across the room, a bank of sinks sat in a row, each with a mirror hung in front, and in that mirror, Roy saw himself, sitting half-naked in a bathroom, panting and pathetic. Less than an hour ago he had been dreaming of this, and now it was happening, all he felt was fear and shame. He stared at his body. What did Sam see in him? Fat. Ugly. Disaster area. Trash. Two months ago had been a fluke, surely. Now, horny and scared, he was paralyzed on this toilet seat, feeling things he had never felt before.

Sam. Sam's face. Sam's body. Sam's ass. Sam's mouth. Roy felt his mouth go dry at the memory of Sam eagerly blowing him. He shivered at the feeling of that little slap and wished he had slapped harder. He breathed hard at the thought of that hard squeeze on his cock.

He wanted Sam.

He stood, slowly, and tucked his cock and balls back into his underwear before zipping up his jumpsuit. He stepped towards the mirror, running his paws under the warm tap water. He stared into his own eyes.

Sam doesn't want you.

He growled and shook his head, reaching up with wet hands to cover his eyes.

I love you, he had said.

No, you don't, Sam had replied.

Those words haunted him. Were they true? Did he…? He found his breathing was quickening again. He was getting worked up. He knew the deal. Sam wanted a quick fuck for the night and Roy was easy, and he didn't have any other plans. That was it. Nothing deeper. No emotions necessary. Roy should get behind that as well. After all, he would have the rabbit's hole all to himself tonight. He had to savor it. Who knew if he would ever even see the man again?

Eyes widened. Teeth clenched. The very thought ran through Roy's chest like a knife and the growl rose up again out of his chest before he closed his eyes. Pain lit up his paw. There was a tinkle of glass shards dropping into the sink, muffled by the sound of the running tap. He opened his eyes and saw the cracks dividing his face a hundred ways, and then looked down at his own paw, clenched into a fist. Shards of glass stuck out of his knuckles. He brushed them off into the sink and ran his hand under the hot tap, making him grunt in pain at the scalding hot water. A little blood mingled with the water and glass in the sink.

Calmer now, Roy turned off the tap, stepped away from the sink, and got a paper towel to dry his hands. His coarse fur covered up the cuts well enough. Bears had thick hides after all. He hardly felt the pain in his knuckles as he dropped the blood-spotted paper towel in the trash before leaving the bathroom.

"What? Did you fall in?" asked Sam, sitting at the table and leaning back in his chair.

"Sorry," said Roy, walking up. He expected to see a plate of food, but instead saw a closed plastic clamshell box in Sam's paw. Sam stood then.

"Seemed kinda late for another drink, and I need a smoke," muttered Sam, thrusting the box into Roy's arms. "Got it to go. We should eat at the hotel to save time."

"Oh... thank you."

"Plus... heh," muttered Sam. He was back to his little

smirks again. Roy longed to see that buck-toothed smile again. "I got a little hot and bothered in there. You didn't jack it in the toilet or something did you? Is that why you took so long?"

"No, I just... had to pee."

"Fine. C'mon."

With that, he began to leave, and Roy followed behind him eagerly.

A fresh shot of fear ran through Roy as they approached the motel, and the bear realized that it was the same motel from two months prior. He looked up as they approached and began to climb up the stairs. He saw that the window he broke was still boarded up. He kept his head down and whispered to Sam.

"Won't people realize we...?"

Sam finished dragging his cigarette and shrugged. "At this dump? A broken window is hardly the worst thing they've ever seen."

With that, Sam put out the smoke in the little ashtray on the cinderblock outside the door, and then got out his key. He turned towards Roy with a cheeky smile as he found the key sitting in his pocket, and the bear couldn't help but laugh a little at the private joke between them. It was going better this time. Much better than two months ago. Roy was more and more at ease, especially after having eaten a few bites of his sandwich and a few fries. When the door opened and Sam held it for him with a cocky smile, Roy entered.

It was a cheap place, with orange shades over the light fixtures casting everything in dingy brown light. There were two beds, but both were big enough that two people could sleep on one. He saw a TV standing on a dresser across from the bed, and at the end of the room was a door leading to a proper bathroom. Roy's eyes went wide. A proper shower – or even a bath – sounded fantastic.

"Home sweet home," joked Sam, flopping down on the bed and kicking off his shoes with a groan. To Roy's surprise, the rabbit had been wearing socks the whole time that matched the color of each tight compression sock to the color of his leg fur – one white and one black. As soon as the bear noticed, Sam looked a little bashful, before he shook one of his ankles and forced a laugh, "Rich living. Doctor's orders, I'm afraid."

"I get it," muttered Roy, nodding as he sat on the other bed and put the box of food on the nightstand between them. "My ankles swell like hell after a long haul. Zero G is hell on your circulation."

"Ugh! I can imagine," muttered Sam, relaxing, before he sat up and hiked up his pant leg. He started to roll one of the socks down his leg slowly, grunting the whole way, before he got it past the ankle and managed to get it all the way off. Then he did the same for the other and gave a deep sigh of relief as he stretched his bare paws. Roy stared at them. They were fuzzier than he expected, but he supposed the man was a rabbit. Without the socks on, he could tell that there was a sagging to the skin under the fur, and as he stared, Sam started to get self-conscious. "Anyway…"

He stood, walking around the bed, before he whipped off his jacket and dug through the pocket. He put a little bottle of lube on the dresser, as well as his roll of condoms, and then tossed the jacket onto a coat rack standing next to it. Roy watched as Sam almost mechanically began to unbutton his shirt. He didn't remember it being like this two months prior. They had been lost in the moment back then – an impromptu encounter. Improvised. Sam hadn't even gotten all his clothes off. This seemed so calculated. Sam was prepared, and all Roy could do was watch and stare as the rabbit took the little bottle of lube and began to step towards the bathroom.

"You finish your sandwich," said the rabbit. "I'll be right

back. Gotta get ready."

Sam disappeared into the bathroom, and soon Roy heard the sink going. Without another thought, he opened the clamshell box back up and continued to eat. It didn't take long for him to finish the last of the fries and sandwich. It wasn't great, but it was good enough. Roy heard a little harsh breath come from the bathroom and wondered what the hell Sam was doing in there.

A moment later, Sam reappeared. He stood in the doorway to the bathroom, leaning against the door frame with a smile on his face. He had stripped off his trousers – and whatever underwear he had been wearing – and had taken off his turtleneck to reveal a tight undershirt, revealing how skinny he was in the chest, neck, and arms. Roy saw the man's hard cock standing at attention. Roy stared hard at him, and Sam seemed to bask in the attention.

"Like what you see?" asked Sam, smiling.

Roy could only nod.

"Good," said Sam, stepping forward and sauntering towards the bed Roy was sitting on. "So?"

"S-So?"

"Why are you still in your clothes?"

Roy looked down and realized that he was, indeed, still in his jumpsuit. He hurried to unzip the company coveralls, but his desperation just made Sam laugh. Soon, gentle paws stopped his own, and Sam began to undress him, slowly. It was almost sweet, seeing the anticipation on Sam's face as he unwrapped Roy like a Christmas present in intricate wrapping paper. Roy was once again powerless, but instead of being held captive by Sam shaming him or manhandling him, he was instead paralyzed by how gentle the rabbit was being. He was being careful. It was so different, not only from two months ago, but from how he had treated the bear in the toilet at the

Riff-Raff.

"S-Sam…" muttered Roy as soon as he was down to his own undershirt and boxer shorts. He reached up to place his paws on Sam's waist, feeling his body through his undershirt. Slowly, wanting to see the rabbit's body, he began to pull up. However, paws on his own stopped him.

"C'mon," said Sam, "Lie back. I'll take charge."

Roy was confused until he felt through the undershirt another stretch of cloth underneath. He remembered that two months back, Sam hadn't even stripped down to his undershirt before.

"Are you wearing something…?" Roy asked, idly.

Sam seemed annoyed and frowned deeply. His cock was flagging slightly, but as he stared at the bear, he seemed to come to some kind of decision and shrugged his shoulders.

"Well… I mean… I try to keep the shirt on," said Sam.

Roy stared into Sam's face, and then his eyes roamed down the rabbit's body, brow furrowed. There was a hunger in the bear's face, Sam realized. A curiosity. Once again, he started tugging the rabbit's undershirt up.

"What are you…? I told you I…"

There, a white, elastic girdle was revealed under the rabbit's undershirt, flattening out the old man's silhouette. Sam fell quiet at this, frowning deeply, and then blushing in clear embarrassment.

"A girdle," Sam said, as if admitting to murder, "I'm getting fat."

"You aren't fat," said Roy, simply, "I'm fat."

Sam rolled his eyes, and said, "You know what I mean. I usually keep it under tighter wraps than this. I'm… I'm not used to sleeping with old farts like you."

"You're older than me."

"Who told you that?" demanded Sam, sounding offended,

suddenly.

"You did."

Sam was silent in answer, realizing that he had let it slip earlier that he was older than Roy. He cleared his throat, before he took the edge of his undershirt and whipped it off over his head. There, he fully revealed the white girdle, made to blend into the rabbit's white fur. He reached behind himself, and with a tearing of Velcro, Sam sighed as the girdle was loosened and then removed.

Sam was still thin. Skeletal in places, actually, with ribs poking through in spots where the fur wasn't as long. It was clear that the man had a naturally thin frame, and Roy figured that he took great pride in that, but his stomach had grown paunchy in his old age, and without the compression around his waist, he had developed a little pot belly. Roy, unused to seeing anyone naked outside the slickly produced bodies of pornography, stared at the rabbit's body in disbelief.

Sam, for a moment, seemed afraid. He was exposed.

"Don't... Don't know why I... why I would..." muttered the rabbit, as Roy's paws began to roam around his body, "I mean... I'm getting heavy around the middle, and..."

"You look beautiful."

Sam blinked his eyes and simply stared. Roy looked up to meet his gaze. He wanted the rabbit so badly. He began to lean forward, his muzzle beginning to hover close to the rabbit's face. A kiss. He wanted to...

However, a sudden pressure stopped him. Sam pushed on his shoulders, and Roy, as if he was a limp doll, fell backwards onto the bed, his own cock straining against his boxers. Sam was done with tender. Through the discomfort of his face, Roy saw the man concentrating on being raunchy and fast, just like he had been in the bathroom of the Riff-Raff. In a smooth, rough movement, he pulled Roy's cock out over the waistband of his boxers and once again dipped down to lick and suck it, making Roy gasp and squirm anew. However, that only lasted for a moment before Sam tore into a condom, rolled it down Roy's thick shaft, and then began to dump lube onto it.

Roy grabbed two fistfuls of sheets as he tried to control his breathing, but the more Sam's paws ran over his dick, the more he couldn't resist the moan that escaped from his muzzle.

Sam smiled wider, and Roy could suddenly see those buck teeth of his. A rush of tenderness washed over him. Cute. Those teeth were cute. As the rabbit climbed on top of him, he felt the rabbit's warm cock rubbing against his belly, and then felt the tip of his own kiss the rabbit's slick entrance.

"We go at my pace," whispered the rabbit, reminding him of the terms, "understood?"

"Y-Yes."

With a nod, the rabbit began to lower himself down onto the bear's cock. He rested his hole against it, breathing deep, and then with a slow, insistent pressure, he pressed down on it. The head of Roy's cock slid in, and the bear gasped. It was happening. It was *happening*!

Roy wanted desperately to thrust up, to bury himself the rest of the way in the rabbit's ass, but he restrained himself. He quivered with anticipation, breathing so hard that he was afraid he was going to hyperventilate, and his paws let go of the sheets to inch towards Sam's legs to take hold of him like he did before. However, the rabbit reached up and slapped his paw away with a smile.

"Bad boy," he said, "You're mine tonight, trash. I decide what to do with you."

There was a throb of his dick, and Sam shivered, getting immediate feedback for his words. He laughed at the sport of it, and slowly lowered himself further, grunting and breathing hard all the way. His own cock softened for a moment until he sat down flush with Roy's lap, and sighed, grimacing in pain, but never losing that wild, buck-toothed smile.

"Fucking pathetic," muttered Sam, out of breath from piercing himself on Roy's cock. "What was that girl's name, Roy?"

"Wh-Wha...?"

"The girl you fucked," said Sam, as he got used to Roy's size, "before you left home. Did she have a name?"

"I... I don't..."

"Can't remember, huh? She didn't even matter to you, did she? You were just trying to prove that you were a man, huh?"

"I..."

"And look at you now," Sam interrupted, wiggling his ass and making Roy grit his teeth. "You wanted me to fuck you earlier. I would have if you weren't so disgusting."

Roy whined, but his cock never softened.

"What kind of man is that?" said Sam. "What's my fucking name?"

"S-Sam?"

"You remembered me, but not her, huh?" the rabbit taunted as he began to lift himself up, making Roy breathe in sharply as his cock was massaged. "Imagine that. I'm the best thing to ever happen to you, big boy, so I better hear some fucking gratitude."

Then, suddenly, Sam lowered himself back down sharply. The rabbit cried out at the feeling of Roy's cock pressing into him, and his own cock suddenly sprang back to life. His paws gripped the folds of Roy's belly fat for leverage, and Roy continued to quiver, unable to move lest Sam disapprove and take away this glorious feeling.

"So?" cried Sam, louder this time, as the exertion of taking it up the ass robbed his voice of its sultry, quiet tone, "I don't hear you."

"Wh-what...?"

Sam then began to bounce his ass up and down, gasping as he did, and Roy's head pressed back against the mattress as he began to roar in sudden, violent pleasure. As he did, Sam, between gasps and pants, continued to talk.

"Some..." *bounce, gasp*, "Fucking," *pant, quiver*, "Gratitude?"

"Th-thank..." Roy began to say, realizing what it was Sam wanted. However, the furious bounce of the rabbit's ass interrupted his words. "Th-thank y... fuck... Oh god..."

"Don't thank God," said Sam sharply, gripping a handful of Roy's fur and pulling. The bear roared in sudden pain. "Thank me."

"Thank you! Oh god! Thank you, S-Sam!" said Roy, his hips moving on their own no matter how much he tried to keep them still. "P...Please? Can... can I...?"

"Fuck me?" asked the rabbit, "After you nearly crushed me last time?"

"I... I won't... oh fuck..." Roy stammered, his mind racing for what he could say to make Sam give him permission, "I'm s-sorry... Thank you! Sam, thank you!"

"Can't resist, can you? Faggot can't wait to fill a man's hole. Bet you want your hole filled too," said Sam, his speech steady now that he was used to the rhythm, although his voice was louder now. "That's an idea. I call up someone who actually wants to touch your nasty hole and have them fuck you for me."

"I... Oh... oh god..."

"I felt that cock jump you pervert," Sam said, one eye closed as he smiled even wider. "I bet I could make you a bottom slut if I wanted to. Too bad too, I'd miss this cock."

Roy had no more words. He simply moaned, and his moans took the shape of a please. His paws hovered in the air, wanting to grab Sam's legs, to control him as he bounced up and down, to fuck up into him, or to roll over and jackhammer into the rabbit like last time. However, he stayed as still as he could.

Sam's eyes darted over to stare at the man's massive paws. It was then that he noticed the cuts and spots of dried blood on the man's right knuckle. Did he cut himself? He remembered Roy destroying that fox two months ago, breaking the window, nearly crushing the life out of the rabbit the first time they fucked. But now he was in control. This man was dangerous, and he was *his*.

Sam's own voice began to grow high pitched and nasally as he too started mumbling, "Oh god... fuck..."

"S-Sam... P-pl..." Roy managed to get out.

"You better fuck me hard," said Sam, eyes flashing dangerously. "Fill me. Prove how much you want me. Prove how much of a good little faggot you are."

"Y-y..." stammered Roy.

However, before he could say anything, Sam reached for his paws and forced them around his own waist. He breathed in, his own cock leaking as it rubbed against Roy's belly, and he felt a thrill of fear, as if he was surrendering himself to being mauled by wildlife. He poised himself with just the man's cockhead in his ass and, bleary-eyed, he gripped the man by the wrists and hissed.

"Fuck," and it carried the air of a command. A command which Roy followed.

Those paws gripped Sam around the midsection and pulled the rabbit down just as those deceptively strong hips thrust up into him. Sam screamed as he was penetrated anew, his head thrown back, and his claws digging into the bigger man's wrists. Then, again and again, Roy drove himself into the rabbit's hole.

It only lasted a few more seconds. After all the teasing, and all the talk, Roy had been wound up like a spring, and his body demanded he push in and out as hard as he could. Sam was suddenly at the bear's mercy as pain lit up his ass anew alongside the pleasure. No more words. No more trash talk. Roy pistoned himself in and out of his rabbit. *His* rabbit. Drool flowed from his open maw. His eyes went unfocused and closed. Sam looked down and saw the ripples in the fat of Roy's belly every time he was brutally slammed down onto the bear's cock.

Then, Roy gasped, crying out more in a squeak than a roar. His eyes opened wide, and then closed again, and he pressed Sam down onto his lap. He shivered, his strokes slowing down as he came hard. Sam reached down to touch himself as he was bounced up and down, and after a few more thrusts of Roy's rapidly softening cock, Sam came as well, leaving streaks of white over the bear's filthy undershirt.

Time was frozen still. Roy and Sam were both breathing hard, muttering and sweating as they came down from their ecstasy. Slowly, Sam began to collapse forward, and Roy let go of his waist, letting him fall. Slowly, the softening bear cock slipped out of the rabbit's ass, and Sam groaned, pressing his face into the bigger man's chest.

"F-Fuck…" muttered Sam, before he laughed. "Ladies and gentlemen, he can be taught."

"Are… Are you…?"

"Never better," said Sam, his tone strangely gentle as his paws went back to running gently across Roy's fur. "Guess we better get some sleep. Maybe a shower."

"I like to shower in the morning," said Roy.

"Makes sense," said Sam, smirking, "I certainly ain't getting up any time soon after that."

Roy laid back, his eyes half-lidded and bleary. His chest was swelling with emotion. He looked down and saw Sam was laying against his belly, eyes closed and face serene, as he seemed to start drifting off to sleep right then and there. However, Roy wasn't ready. Roy had more to say.

"S-Sam…"

"Don't fucking say it."

"I… I wasn't going to."

Sam's annoyed scowl broke the sweet serenity of the moment as he opened his eyes.

"What then?"

Roy hesitated for only a moment before he reached back to Sam's sides and lifted him up. As if he weighed nothing, Sam was dragged across Roy's chest, until their muzzles were inches apart, and then a whisper from one another.

The kiss wasn't anything special. Roy simply brushed the tip of his snout across the tip of Sam's, and for a moment, there was bliss. The two of them lay, pressing their snouts together, eyes closed, reveling in that brief, beautiful moment of connection. Sam even pressed his own snout deeper, losing himself for a moment, and Roy felt the flick of a tongue asking to be let in. He parted his muzzle, and soon they kissed for real, for the first time in Roy's life.

Sam jerked away suddenly, blinking his eyes hard. He stared hard into Roy's face, and Roy, with a thrill of joy, recognized something there. Tenderness. Perhaps, Love? Was he getting through to the rabbit? Was this going to be more than just a hurried night of fucking.

Sam's face grew blank, and he said, flatly, "You have to leave."

"Wh-What?"

Sam pulled away from their embrace, stood up and started to gather up his clothes. He picked up his compression socks, his girdle, his own undershirt, and the jacket on the coat rack, and as he did, said, "You have an apartment with The Company. You can go sleep there."

"B-But... what? Why? I..." stammered Roy as he sat up.

"I'm filthy," muttered Sam, "I better take a shower now. You can let yourself out. Don't fucking break anything."

And with that, Sam walked into the bathroom, closed the door, and Roy could hear the lock turn over. A moment later, the water began to flow, and he heard the shower.

Roy laid back, stunned. Leave? Now? What about the kiss? What about their shower in the morning? Was he bad? Did he fuck up?

He laid there for several minutes, cum drying into his undershirt and belly fur, before he finally stood up. He found his discarded jumpsuit and hoped that would cover up the stench of sex enough for him to walk back to the company apartment bloc. He sat to put his boots back on, and finally turned to leave.

Would he never see Sam again?

He turned back, staring at the bathroom door. A wild thought suddenly came over him. An urge. The door was flimsy. The lock was cheap. His boots were sturdy. He could kick it down. He could break the door down, run in, join Sam, and... and what? Surely that wouldn't help. Surely Sam would scream at him, but... but he would be naked. Wet. After he had done so well, Sam was brushing him off. He could keep proving himself. He imagined the rabbit in the shower, water running down his black and white fur, clinging to his already skinny frame. He was so vulnerable. Roy could do whatever he wanted.

Roy found himself growing hard again, but after the hard fucking, his balls ached. He took a few steps towards the door, closer and closer, eyes drilling into the doorknob where he knew a few swift kicks was all that was between him and *his rabbit*.

However, he caught himself before he did something that

he would regret. He instead put a gentle paw on the door, and then knocked.

"Goodnight, Sam," he said, "see you... in two months?"

There was no answer; only the sound of the shower. Roy nodded his head, turned away from the bathroom door, and walked out of the motel room.

THIRD ENCOUNTER:
FABULA GALAXY

A young piece of ass was waving in front of Sam's face. He leaned back and took a sip of his drink – vodka soda with a twist of lime – and let the kid work. The body *moved*, and the rabbit had to appreciate that. The man's muscular back contracted as he reached his arms up to rest behind his head. His fat ass had a good wobble to it, and the young horse's silky tail waved across his face and dipped down to brush across his lap. Sam nodded. The smell of sweat and cologne made his lip curl, and the cheer of the crowd was almost enough to drown out the pumping music.

The kid was probably twenty-two, if Sam had to guess. College age at least, but by the calm, business-like look on the horse's face as he gave the rabbit a lap dance, he had been doing this already for a long time. Sam took another drink, being careful to keep the horsehair tail out of his vodka.

Laughter erupted around him. He had found himself sitting at one of the VIP balconies up above, where a bunch of young dudes from the colony college – maybe classmates of the horse – were jeering and cheering Sam on as he calmly nodded along with the graceful but professional lap dance. It wasn't Sam's first. That had been a long time ago. It was unlikely to be his last. That these kids thought it was funny to buy a treat for 'daddy' annoyed him.

The thong came down and Sam had an unobstructed view of the horse's ass. A cheer rose up as the horse dipped down, twerking his thick haunches over the rabbit's lap, merely brushing against the front of the man's pants. Sam, knowing what he would see, looked around. Several of the young bucks he was spending the night with were chanting along with the rhythmic clap of the horse's cheeks, but others were simply staring, wide-eyed. One in particular, a white-furred jock of a dog, maybe the same age as the horse, was mesmerized by that ass.

Sam finally cracked a smile.

"Hey Greg," said Sam, "like what you see?"

The dog stammered, blinking hard, and the rest of his friends laughed at this clear call-out. Several arms found their way around the dog's shoulders, shaking him and making him remember where he was. Sam knew this group was about even split between bros who were here as a joke, and closet cases who were hopelessly in love with someone on the football team or whatever. This club was about the only openly queer place on the whole station – a bar during the afternoon and a strip club and drag venue at night – and its proximity to the campus meant it was common for fratboys to dare each other to go spend the evening drinking in Fabula Galaxy. It was so common as to be suspicious, in Sam's opinion, and he found that he was often just as likely to take the darer back to his hotel as the dare-ee.

Greg was a special case. Sam actually recognized Greg from his father's planetside import business, and they did a lot of work together as well as for The Company. They were also unapologetic queer-bashers, and Sam had to spend a lot of time keeping all of this on the lowdown. To find their dar-ling baby boy here, staring with such an obvious hunger at the stripper's big ass, was just too delicious not to shoot his shot.

He reached into his pocket and pulled out a tip once he sensed that the horse was winding down his dance, and smoothly stuffed the bills between the horse's asscheek and the string of his thong. He then, however, pulled out another crisp bill and offered it to the horse. Not enough for a lap dance, but he knew he was well within his right to ask for a little extra for a tip.

"Maybe show my friend Greg here a little show as well, with my thanks," said Sam, smoothly, and the horse, showing the first personality he had shown since he started dancing, plastered a sultry look on his face as he turned to glare at Greg.

The dog froze, his face falling. The horse strode up with his thong just barely holding in his cock, and he bent his knees to drop to the floor in front of Greg, before slowly picking him-self back up, putting his snout right next to Greg's confused erection clearly visible through his pants. The dancer stood up until his horse cock dangled over the guy's lap, and then hov-ered over his face. Sam was impressed at how smoothly that thong could slip on and off to show off the goods. Greg, in a moment of weakness, reached up to touch that fleshy spire, but the horse reached down and slapped him gently.

"No touching," the horse said, voice even and unromantic. "That's it, boys."

To the jeers of the college kids, the stripper walked on, but Sam only had eyes for Greg and the deep red blush that was no doubt showing through his white fur. If they weren't being lit with blues and pinks, Sam was sure he would have seen it. After a moment, the college party went back to their business of drinking and planning out new ways to tease the old timer they had invited up to the VIP balcony 'as a joke,' but Greg soon locked eyes with Sam, and Sam, likewise locked eyes with the dog. He was horny, and drunk, and ready to make some bad decisions.

"Well, boys," said Sam, standing up, "It's been fun, but I should really get back to the party downstairs."

"Y-You're leaving already?" asked Greg, standing up as well. He was taller than Sam.

"I know when I'm being treated as a joke, plus I need a smoke," said Sam, before he waved to the rest of the assembled college hoodlums. "At least one of you knows how to treat a gentleman."

"Well, good to, uh, meet you, Sam," said Greg, and in those words, Sam heard a whole host of other things he would have wanted to say. Instead, he offered a paw for the rabbit to shake.

Sam smirked and surreptitiously slipped one of his personal cards into his palm before he took the dog's hand. The boy felt the paper get pushed into his palm, and as Sam turned to walk away, he knew the boy would be blushing even harder as he realized he had just gotten the number of one of the old greymuzzle queers that they had come to gawk at. Maybe it wouldn't lead to anything. Maybe it would end in a night of curious sex. Either way, Sam was satisfied as he walked down out of the VIP balcony, gave a nod to the bouncer, and made his way out the front door and out into the cool night.

He breathed the recycled air of the colony as he looked up and saw the dark projected sky above. One in the morning. Something was nagging at the back of his mind, but he ignored it. He lit up a cigarette and wandered over to an area off to the side of the entrance to Fabula where a couple gothy looking tenderqueers were passing a vape back and forth. He didn't pay them much mind and they didn't pay him much mind either. He leaned against the wall in the smoking area and sighed out a lungful of calming smoke.

"H-Hey!" came a familiar voice and Sam smiled. He turned and saw Greg.

The white dog actually had some patches of tan and grey throughout his coat, but he was still mostly shock white and wore a tight tee shirt and baggy pants. By his physique he probably played some sport, and jackpot sirens were firing in Sam's head. He'd isolated himself from the rest of his group. Sam silently thanked mothers everywhere for forgetting to teach their sons what their daughters learned well – there's strength in numbers.

"Hello Gregory," said Sam, trying to sound formal. He had a persona to play to: Daddy.

"S-Sam, uh, hi," said the dog. "You, uh, smoke?"

"Do you?"

"N-Not really, I… I just wanted to, uh…" stammered the dog. He had no game – or at least wasn't used to having to try his game on a member of the same sex. All the better for Sam to take charge.

"When we go back in there, would you like to buy me a drink?" asked Sam.

"Huh? Oh! S-sure…"

"Maybe go somewhere else and get to know each other," muttered Sam, moving closer to the college kid, enjoying the look of sudden worry on the dog's face. "After all, those friends of yours are pretty loud and rowdy. I know a quiet spot nearby."

"O-Oh… I… I mean…" Greg continued to mutter, before he said, quietly, "I'm not gay."

"What are you doing out here talking to me then?"

"I just… I mean… you gave me your card and I… I thought I should… give it back?"

Pathetic, thought Sam, *but adorable.* "Keep it, in case you ever wanted to get hold of me. After all, gay, straight, who cares long as it feels good, right?"

"R-Right, sure…" he said, eyes wide, "Where's… Where's that spot?"

"You all cashed out?"

"My friends were covering the tab."

Sam nodded, and started walking, gesturing for the boy to follow. With tail wagging, the kid followed along, and Sam couldn't help but laugh. One of the easier catches he's had, ever since Morty spread around to all the baby gays at the college that Daddy Sam was a jerk. But the squads of fratboys in denial? There wasn't too much crossover there.

Sam walked along with Greg catching up to him, and together they wandered away from the club and towards the nondescript door where Sam knew the Riff-Raff to be hidden away. The kid wouldn't care about the ugly shag carpet or the terrible service. He was horny and confused, and Sam wasn't about to let someone like that get away.

However, as Sam put a hand on the door leading down to the basement where the Riff-Raff sat, Sam felt a twitch of his ears and followed the instinct, looking around. There, he recognized a shape in the darkness, coming up the street behind them. A man – a tall man, thickset and round, who was walking up the street behind them. As soon as Sam turned to stare, the man stopped, remaining in the darkness between the streetlamps, and the rabbit narrowed his eyes.

"Bar's downstairs," he said, going first. If someone was stalking them, better the strapping young lad get stabbed before him.

Greg was disappointed as he stepped into the Riff-Raff, but not surprised. Another reason why a good number of the fratboys ended up at Fabula was because it was one of the only bars worth a damn in the neighborhood. Little holes in the wall like this were all over the place, and everyone who drinks had been to at least two or three before the ambiance chased them away. On the other hand, nowhere else was better than this to make conversation or to have a quick fuck and suck in the bathroom without anyone caring.

Vodka soda and a beer. Despite himself, Sam smiled. It was just like…

He cleared his throat as they sat down at a corner booth – facing away from the TV so neither of them would be distracted – and at once, Sam leaned towards the young man he had managed to lure here.

"So, what are you studying?" he asked – a surefire ice breaker.

"Uh… exoplanet geology," he answered. Sam pretended to be impressed. Seb U was known for being a great school for that, considering the mining colony was attached to a treasure trove of surrounding, ore-rich moons, as well as the 'exciting' field of harvesting gasses from the atmosphere of the planet. Every other one of these brats was majoring in exogeology.

"Sounds interesting," said Sam after a drink, "Do you like it?"

"Well… kinda. Dad insisted," muttered the boy. "He doesn't want me to end up like him, I guess."

"Like what?"

"Working a dead-end job," said the boy. "He wants me to get a good company job. Planetside surveyor, or something in R&D. Anything to stay out of buying and selling shit."

Sam controlled his face. He 'bought and sold shit' just like Greg's father. He held his tongue. He'd pay that back when the kid was underneath him begging.

"Well, good luck with that," said Sam, keeping the warm, fatherly tone. The daddy issues were certainly there, ripe for the picking, "Anything you'd rather be doing?"

"I'm... I'm on the lacrosse team, actually!" the boy said, lighting up at once, "Coach says I could go pro if I want..."

However, before the kid could finish his answer, there was a sudden noise from the bartender. "You. Out."

Sam looked up and saw that the old wolf at the bar was pointing a finger towards the door. His face was grey stone as he scowled towards whoever had just walked into the Riff-Raff. On any other day, Sam would have just went back to talking to Greg and forgotten all about it, but the sight of that shadowy figure outside made him wonder. He turned to look.

His eyes widened as he saw the massive man standing, agitated, in the bar as the bartender yelled at him to leave. The bear was looking around desperately, and the wolf kept yelling, "Get the fuck out of here!"

Then, Roy's eyes darted across Sam's booth, and they locked eyes. Roy. Sam's breathing caught in his throat. It had been two months since then, of course. It had slipped his mind. Roy was back in town.

"Sam? You alright?" asked Greg, who was looking from Sam to Roy.

"No," said Sam, "We have to go."

Sam stood, forgetting his drink. As soon as he did, Roy started to cry out, "Sam!"

"Come on Greg, we'll find somewhere else."

"Sam! Hey!" cried the bear as he strode up to the rabbit. The bartender gave a growl.

"Last chance fucker! Don't think I don't remember you breaking one of my fucking mirrors last time you were in here."

Sam paused, looking up at Roy, but only for a moment. He had to pass by the bear to get out of the bar, and as he did, he had taken Greg by the paw to guide him out with him. He hoped Roy wouldn't start anything. He wanted Roy to shut up and disappear. However, as he tried to walk on by, he felt a heavy paw on his shoulder.

"Sam. Hi."

"Let go of me, Roy. I'm busy today."

"I… I just got in. I looked for you," said the bear, desperation dripping from him. "Then I saw you walking here and…"

Sam tried to shrug the bear's paw off his shoulder. However, the bear's grip only tightened.

"Let go of me!"

"Sam, who the fuck is this?" asked Greg, taking on an aggressive stance as he squared up to the bear. After all, Sam was Greg's date, after a fashion. Sam nodded, sure that he could use the kid to get out of this.

Roy ignored Greg and stared at Sam.

"That's it! Out!" cried the bartender, pulling a long, thick bat out from under the bar. "Fucking out if you want to keep your knees."

Roy finally glanced over at the bartender and started to step out, as if he was accompanying Sam towards the door. Sam, however, planted his feet and tried to resist it, but was dragged physically across the carpet.

"Let go!"

"Sam, we have to go," said Roy. "I wanted to see you."

"I don't want to fucking see you!" he screamed.

Greg finally stepped in, the white knight to the rescue. "Let go of him, man!"

The dog pushed Roy, who barely moved, and the bear slowly turned to stare at the dog. Sam realized that he had seen that look before. Memories of broken glass and of the fox writhing on the floor of the Waffle Station invaded his mind. If the bartender hadn't run up with his bat held high, threatening to beat the hell out of Roy, Sam was sure Greg was dead, and by the hard, frightened look on Greg's face, he had seen the same alternate future.

Roy, finally let go, retreating from the bat and ran out the door with only a sad glance towards Sam. The bartender followed him out, no doubt to make sure he wasn't going to hang around by the entrance. Greg stood, eyes wide, and Sam, for his part, was empathetic enough to reach up to touch the kid on the shoulder.

"Thanks, sport," said Sam with a smile, trying to pick up the 'daddy' routine where they left off, but Greg was having none of it. He stared at the door, and then at Sam, before he started to leave himself.

"N-Nice to meet you, mister," he said, retreating from unfamiliar territory, "I... I think I better go find my friends."

"Oh, come on! That was just an old..." Sam nearly said boyfriend, but stopped himself, "...some guy who can't take 'no.' I'm still ready to go if you are."

"N-No. I had better..."

Greg was leaving, and Sam followed him up the stairs and out into the open air.

Sam, sounding more desperate than he wanted to, tossed a Hail Mary, "I've got a hotel room for the night. You're hot stuff, and..."

"N-No thanks!" Greg said, and as soon as he was out in the open, he began to power-walk down the street, not even saying goodbye. Sam raised a hand to try to stop him and call out to him, but he knew he'd never be able to catch him, and by the time he got back to Fabula, the others would have either left or would have shunned him for trying to fuck one of their boys. Sam instead slapped his paw on his forehead, giving a frustrated growl.

Fucking Roy! Goddamn it!

A smoke. He needed a smoke. Fuck it, the mood was off today. He lit one up and turned away from Fabula. Fuck the hotel room. Fuck the bars. Fuck trying to scrounge up some bedwarmer for the night. He was done. It was going to be expensive, but he wanted to spend the night at home. A rideshare, then, back to his home, and he would have to figure out some new stomping grounds. With both the baby gays and the jocks on to him, this neighborhood had been tainted.

He wandered off towards the docks where he knew the rideshares would be congregating this time of night, but as he passed an alley, his fur stood on end. He glanced to one side and saw the massive shape of a bear lurking in the darkness.

"Fuck!" he cried, startled. "You want me to fucking piss myself, Roy?"

The bear stepped into the light of the streetlamps. His eyes were wide and wet. Sam stared at them and made his own eyes hard. He wanted to walk away – *run* away. Roy had crossed a line, and Sam thought he respected himself too much to keep anyone like that around. However, even as he thought that, something kept him rooted to the spot.

"What the fuck were you thinking?" Sam said after a moment, reaching up to swat the bear on the arm as hard as he could, which wasn't particularly hard at all.

"I wanted to see you," said Roy.

Sam snorted, furrowing his brow and tossing his cigarette on the ground, not even bothering to stomp it out.

"We've been over this, Roy," he said in a voice that was low, even, and careful. "I am not your boyfriend. We are not seeing each other. You were a couple of one-night stands that I am coming to regret more and more every time I see you."

"The... that last time was... was good. I..."

"Get over yourself," Sam muttered with a sneer. "I don't give a shit about the sex. It was just fucking sex, whatever. What I give a shit about is you following me around like a lovesick puppy. I don't go for that, Roy. This isn't about feelings. I just wanted to get my dick wet. I got what I wanted, and I don't want anything else from you."

With that, Sam turned and kept going, but he heard the heavy footsteps of Roy's boots following him. With a snarl, the rabbit turned and continued to yell.

"Get the fuck away from me!"

"I... I don't... I wanted to see you. I thought... I thought you and I were..."

"Well, you thought wrong. Don't follow me."

"The way you looked at me..." muttered Roy. "The way you... you kissed me..."

"*You* kissed *me*, Roy, and I didn't ask you to, either."

"You... You didn't complain. You kissed me back."

"I... fuck..." Sam said, burying his face in his hands, "It's been an awful day, Roy. You cockblocked me – for the second time now, I might add – and now you won't. Fucking. Go. Away."

"I'm just... confused, is all," said Roy. "Can't we go somewhere? Can't we talk?"

"There's nothing to talk about."

"There is! I... I want us to..."

"And I don't! There, we talked! It takes two to tango, Roy, and I am flying solo tonight, so goodnight and good-fucking-bye."

Sam turned then, resolute in his intention not to turn around until he was safe inside one of those rideshares heading back to his part of town. His stomach fluttered in fear. He was alone on the street and Roy... he didn't know what Roy was going to do. All Sam had to do was walk away. There was nothing else he could do. What was he supposed to do if Roy got violent? Fight him? Run? Nerves began to fray as he put one foot in front of the other.

That was when he heard the roar behind him. He should have broken into a run. He should have pulled out his house-keys to gouge the fucker's eyes out. Instead, he turned, a thrill of excitement running through him as he heard a loud impact.

Roy was leaning against an aluminum-sided wall, his face covered by one enormous paw, while the other, balled up into a fist, had left a deep dent in the siding. Roy was wracked with sobs as he picked up his fist, and it, once again, impacted with the wall, denting it further. The sheer strength in the big bear's limbs was such that Sam was sure he was going to put his fist through the wall.

Then, the fingers over his face parted, and Sam saw a glimpse of those brown eyes, wide and flush with tears and staring at the rabbit with a clear, violent hunger.

"F-Fuck this!"

Sam broke into a run, putting distance between himself and the huge, violent man. He soon found himself out of breath, but the adrenaline kept him going for several blocks until a stitch in his side forced him to stop. He was within sight of the docks – a ship-park on the outskirts of the station where freight ships, rideshare taxis, and joyriding yachts were resting. Even this late at night, it was busy here. The Company always had someone hauling things here or there, and at the very least Sam could take solace from the presence of other people. Safety in numbers. He had to laugh, and the laugh caused his side to ache anew.

He limped forward, heart still beating way too fast, until the streetlights over the ship docks were bright and he could hear the voices of people working the night shift. Nearby he saw a bank of cabs – black, boxy flying vehicles, each of which had a driver leaning against the side swiping a tablet in aloof boredom as they waited for a new mark – and knew he was safe.

That fucking bear, thought Sam as he took a moment to catch his breath. He found a bench near the rideshares and collapsed onto it, breathing in and out to lower his heart rate. His doctor warned him about his high blood pressure, and of course he heard the nagging of the old puma about quitting smoking. He thought, for a moment, if he hadn't smoked so much, he might have been able to run longer.

That bear. He was crazy. Obsessive. Dangerous. The sex was bad, the company was worse. He was a bore, a sad sack, and was only good for hauling freight and causing property damage. Sam thought he must have been the dumbest mother-fucker in the world to see the bear a second time after that first one. He wasn't even sure why. He never had to see Roy again after that first fuck. He sought him out two months ago. Why? If he hadn't done that, he wouldn't be in this mess now.

There was a very real danger, Sam realized, that he could have died if he stayed by Roy's side.

The thought made Sam's breath catch in his throat. The cuts on his knuckles; he had seen them while they were fuck-ing. He'd also seen the broken mirror in the Riff-Raff. He hadn't figured out why they were there until the bartender came at them with that bat. Roy broke it. Why? Because he was so wound up and didn't know where else to put all those emotions? Because he was frustrated when Sam didn't finish sucking his dick? First, a window, then a mirror, now a wall, and next... Sam reached up to feel his own neck.

And then down, to fondle himself through the front of his trousers. He clenched his jaw. Really? *Really?* It must have been the excitement. The adrenaline. He wasn't getting hard at the thought of Roy roughing him up. He wasn't. He couldn't be.

But then the thought of the fox moaning on the ground came to mind.

You knew what he was the whole time, Sam thought to himself. *That was why you wanted him from the start.*

"As if," he said out loud, leaning back and reaching for his cigarettes. However, he found an empty pack and breathed out sharply as he crumpled it up. Of course. One more thing to add to the pile.

He stood then, intending to go hire a cab and be done with that night, but then he felt his erection pressing against the front of his underwear, and gave a small gasp.

Without consciously understanding why, he turned away from the cabs and towards the company lot. There was only one freighter that was parked in the lot this time of night. All the rest were either on the way in or out. Only one stood unmanned and ignored – a red, snub-nosed ship with a massive cargo train behind it, which had already been unloaded and reloaded with tomorrow's freight for Roy to haul. Sam reached up to touch his neck again. He couldn't possibly be considering…?

He walked towards the company lot. He opened his wallet and pulled out the company ID he had from work and pressed it to the reader on the fence. There was a beep, a green light, and suddenly he was walking towards Roy's freighter, hands in his pockets with eyes wide.

This is a good way to get murdered, he thought to himself. *He is waving every red flag.*

Sam found that he had no answer to that.

It's only going to get worse. He's going to be insufferable. He's going to follow you around forever. He's going to ruin your life.

"Maybe…" he muttered.

A thrill of fear went through him. He felt like he was standing on the edge of a cliff as he approached the ship. It had been cleaned, but it was still dinged from minor collisions in space, and the color was faded on one side from the solar radiation. The door to the ship's airlock stood, locked, and the handle was flush to the body of the ship, presumably until Roy came around to unlock it. However, there was a small seam between the door and the frame.

It's been a long time since anyone loved you as much as Roy loves you.

He paused, staring at the door, and clenched his jaw. He was afraid that Roy would appear, or that someone from security would come around and ask him what he was doing here so late. What was he even here to do? Wait all night for him? Talk to him in the morning?

Sam was astonished at how hard he was, thinking about that fat freighter, his thick paws, and thicker thighs, and all the violence he could do. Was he alright with that? Was he that bored with his life that he was willing – no, eager – to risk it for *him* of all people?

Sam didn't have an answer, at least not one he was willing to admit to himself, and as he stepped forward and slipped his business card into the seam of the door until it stuck out from the faded red, he clenched his jaw tighter. However, he kept his fingers tightened around the little card, and soon pulled it back out before he reached into another pocket and found a ballpoint pen he had stolen from Fabula when he signed his receipt.

You are going to learn boundaries.
-Sam

Then, he placed the card where Roy would see it and, quickly, walked away. The bear had his number now, and Sam didn't have to think about the consequences of that for another two whole months.

Soon after, Sam found his way into the back of a rideshare, flew back home, and in bed, slowly stroked himself off to the thought of those fierce, hungry eyes, and huge claws tearing him apart.

Fourth Encounter:
Lucky Bowl

Hi.

Hello? Sam?

Who the fuck is this???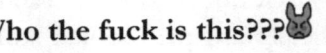

It is Roy. Sebastin Station route. We met at
Waffle Station.

*Sebastian

Oh

Hello Roy.

There's a bowling alley here.

I am aware.

I'm coming in earlier than usual. Light lod. Ahead of schedule. Thout maybe you wanted to go bowling.

*thought

*load

Ill give you a load alright 🐰

🐰Anyway that place is for kids, isnt it?

I haven't been bowling since I was a kid.

🐰🐰🐰🐰🐰🐰

Thats almost cute

Or we could go somewhere else.

I want to see you.

I'm better this time.

If you don't want to see me that's okay.

I'll shut up.

Hello?

What the hell  when

8? They close at 10.

Do they serve liquor there?

Yes, I think so.

See you at 8, big guy

Dont be a fuck this time

Ok.

LMAO What are you doing?

I didn't know what it meant but you did it
so I decided to do it too is that bad?

Your a fucking idiot
Read, 6:45pm

Sam was sure the Lucky Bowl had been here since the station had been built a couple hundred years ago. The décor was quaint – that is to say, several decades out of date – and by the crowd of Roy, Sam, the guy at the counter and two bored looking teenagers two lanes over, it was clear that it was a slow night. Maybe even a slow decade, considering the paint peeling from the corners of the room and the ever-present smell of old fried food and stale beer.

Roy, however, was more enthusiastic about this trip than he had been for any of their others. Something came to life when Roy walked into that dated building, eyes widened, and as they rented their shoes and picked out a lane, he was practically bouncing.

They didn't talk much at first. Sam made some perfunctory small talk. After that, Roy focused on the game, and Sam, who was immediately lousy at it and grew bored and frustrated at once, decided to instead focus on Roy.

The bear was wearing something other than his work outfit. It seemed that he'd arrived at Seb very early indeed, and he had taken the time to change into a more casual outfit for their 'date,' if you could even call it that. He wore a flannel shirt, formless khaki pants, and a wide-brimmed cap with a cartoon chipmunk on it that Sam vaguely recognized as a mascot for some fuel station. He looked like an old Earth lumberjack.

Sam, on the other hand, wore a blue windbreaker over a collared shirt, and his most comfortable pair of slacks. He figured that since Roy had already seen him naked and wanted to see more, it wouldn't matter what he wore, and dressing up for the bowling alley seemed gauche, so he dressed casually.

A couple pins bounced around violently as Roy picked up another spare. He wasn't great at the game by any means, but he was a damn sight better than Sam was. The rabbit was leaning forward, staring at the bear's broad back, and vaguely wondering when this was going to be over. There were five frames left to go, and already the score was so uneven that Sam doubted he would ever be able to catch up with the amount of gutter balls he was throwing.

At least there was beer. No liquor, unfortunately, but the selection of beers was at least inoffensive enough that Sam had something cold to sip while he waited his turn. Roy sat down next to him on an orange molded plastic chair and smiled.

"Your turn," he said.

Sam stared at him. The smile seemed alien on the big bear's

face. Sam realized he had never really seen Roy happy before. He'd seen him depressed, in the throes of passion, and when he was about to destroy something, but never a proper smile. Sam, amazingly enough, matched the smile and shrugged.

"It's like eighty-two to nine, you're kicking my ass," said Sam.

"You could still catch up."

"Meh," the rabbit grunted, before he took a drink. He drained his bottle then, and stood up. "How about another round?"

"Er... Sam?" asked Roy, his smile beginning to fade. "Are you having fun?"

Sam stared at the bear, before he shrugged and said, "Well, yeah. I'm just lousy at it."

"Let me finish mine before you get more beers," said Roy, reaching for his own bottle and taking a sip. "Maybe... we could take a break from the game? Do something else?"

Sam paused before he gave a deep sigh, and sat back down, "Yeah, whatever."

"Last time I went bowling, I was probably... sixteen. Planetside on Mars. Much nicer place than this. Crowded. Same carpets though."

"I think they shipped those carpets all across the system forty years ago," muttered Sam, staring down at the tight-weave carpet with printed shapes on it, "and haven't gotten a new shipment since."

"Yeah..."

"I guess I was... maybe twelve when I bowled? With my dad, and a couple friends," Sam said, shrugging.

"Oh. I went alone."

"You bowled... alone?"

Roy's mood soured at once, and he nodded. "I didn't know a lot of people growing up. Nobody really liked me much. I was… big. Kids made fun of me."

"Whoof," said Sam, frowning. "Sad."

"I didn't… I mean, when I picked this place I… I dunno. I wasn't really thinking about it. There were probably better places to go, but it sounded fun so…"

"Don't make excuses," snapped Sam, tapping his bottle on the tabletop, "It's fine. I'm having fun."

"Good!" said Roy, trying to make himself sound excited, before he repeated, "Good."

"After this, we should find somewhere to eat that serves something other than corn dogs and soda," said Sam, glancing at the food kiosk with some light disdain.

"Yeah," said Roy.

Silence fell over the table. Sam stared at the last dregs of Roy's beer, waiting for him to finish them. However, the bear was lost in thought, staring at the table and swishing the liquid around the bottom of the bottle.

"Sam," said the bear, finally, and asked, "I scared you last time, didn't I?"

Sam looked up into his face, furrowing his brow, before he slowly answered, "Clearly not enough for me to run off, I guess."

"I get like that… sometimes," explained Roy. "I've been lonely. I didn't want to be alone that day."

"Yeah, so you said."

"But I scared you, so…" he said. "S-Sorry."

The rabbit stared for another moment, blinking his eyes, before he nodded his head. Without any words coming, Roy continued.

"And," he said, "thanks. For your card, I mean. I'm… I'll… I want to…"

"Drop it," muttered Sam in a low deadpan. "Drink your beer."

Roy followed the order immediately, knocking back the rest of his drink and handing the empty bottle to Sam. The rabbit smiled pleasantly as he stood up and walked away.

Two more beers were ordered, and Sam stood awkwardly by the kiosk, as if he was considering buying something else. He could sense that Roy was trying to make deeper conversation and the rabbit was wasting time before that could continue. In all honesty, Sam was having fun in a strange way. It had been a long time since he'd gone someplace quiet, and it had been a long time since someone had been so interested in him and desperate to please him. Oh sure, the younger fellows wanted 'Daddy's' approval, but Sam knew that was never about him. Those kids were fucking him because they had issues and Sam happened to be the nearest old fart they could take it out on. Roy was different. Not that he didn't have issues, he did. And the issues might have been worse, to be honest, but they were... new. Different issues at least. The novelty appealed to Sam, but at the same time he was having trouble trying to figure out how to handle it.

He wasn't used to confronting sincerity, and Roy, for all his faults, was absolutely honest.

Eventually, Sam took the beers and delivered them back to the bear, who was still seated on the plastic chair.

"Last round here I think," said Sam. "I'm starting to get hungry. Let's finish the game and get going. I think..."

"Sam," said Roy, suddenly. He did not look up at the rabbit.

"What now?" Sam said, annoyance in his tone, but he waited for Roy to talk.

Roy paused for only an instant, before he said, "You should be more scared of me, shouldn't you?"

He glanced up to meet Sam's eyes, but didn't have the courage to hold his gaze, instead dipping down to stare at the beer in his paw.

Sam let the moment lie, unsure of what to say except to twist off the cap of the bottle and take a swig. Roy took that as his signal to continue.

"Everybody's always been scared of me," he said, voice quiet. "I've always... been... like this. I always break things. When I was a kid, I was fat and ugly, and everyone made fun of me, and then I was tall and got stronger, and everyone was scared of me, and nobody ever... ever wanted to talk to me."

"Didn't you used to run with larger crews of freighters?"

"I liked them, but... I was always quiet, and nobody really tried to get to know me."

"Well, shit," said Sam, eyes half-lidded as he tried to figure out what to say, "That sucks."

"Yeah," said Roy, "So... are you...? Scared of me, I mean?"

Sam paused, before he took another drink and sat down next to him.

"You're fucking scary, yeah," said Sam. "You nearly put your fist through a solid wall last time I saw you."

Roy flinched, his shoulders tensing.

"But... ugh..." Sam said. "Look, I'm going to be honest, I probably shouldn't have given you my card."

"Oh. You... you don't have to..."

"Shut the fuck up and listen," snapped Sam. "Yeah, I'm scared of you, and that kind of... turns me on? I dunno."

"Oh," said Roy, turning his face to stare into Sam's eyes. They took on a slightly wild look, and Sam felt a now familiar thrill of fear within. "You know you can do whatever you want to me, y'know? Call me whatever you want. I don't mind. I just... I don't want to be alone anymore. Nights with you are the only thing... the only thing I'm looking forward to anymore. I feel like I'm going to go insane if I don't see you."

Sam furrowed his brow, before he sneered, shaking his head in disbelief.

"That's the most pathetic thing I've ever heard."

"It's the truth though."

"That's what makes it so pathetic," the rabbit said, leaning back. "You latched on to me? Me of all people. Do you even know who I am?"

"You're... Sam."

"I'm a fucking jerkoff is who I am," the rabbit said, throwing an arm around the back of Roy's chair as he spoke. "A player. An asshole. I got divorced once, and I have no intention of committing to anything else. I'm fifty-six years old, and goddamn it, I wish I was still twenty-two and knew what I knew at thirty-five. Nothing has ever really been good or exciting for me since then, and the only way I can get my kicks is by using people. You're the one who should be turning around and running away."

"I don't mind. I'm forty-five. You're not that much older than me."

"Feels like I am," muttered Sam, "And it feels like I should be running too, but... your ugly ass is probably the most interesting thing that's happened to me in a decade at least. Isn't that sad?"

Roy paused, staring at Sam for a moment, before he asked, "You really mean that?"

"Don't make me say it again," said Sam, reaching up to cover his eyes with a paw. "Both of us need to fucking run away from each other as fast and as far as we can. We don't need this. We need fucking therapy."

"Sorry."

"Whatever," said Sam, glancing over. "You can make it up to me."

"O-Oh..."

"Drink your beer," said Sam, and after the bear took a drink, he leaned forward and continued, "You want to be with me?"

"Y-Yes."

"Fine," muttered Sam, scooting his butt to the edge of his own plastic chair so that their thighs were touching. "Then let's talk about the rules."

"R-Rules?"

"After last time, hell yeah, rules," muttered Sam. "First, you ever fucking hit me, I'm out. Period."

"O-okay."

He scooted a little closer, reaching down with a hand to run it along the inside of Roy's thigh. Roy's eyes widened and he looked around. The bored teenagers had left, and the guy at the kiosk wasn't paying attention.

"Second, no stalking me either or showing up unannounced. You text me like you did today, like a good boy, you get a treat. Understood?"

With that, Sam's hand ran up the bear's lap and latched tight onto his cock through his khakis. Roy jumped, eyes wide and jaw dropped, as he was fondled openly in public.

"S-Sam... someone... someone's going to s-see..."

"Third," Sam said, ignoring the bear's words. "You and me are not boyfriends, lovers, or in love, and there will be no discussion of marriage or moving in together or anything else. This is about sex first, companionship a distant third or fourth. I don't care how shitty your childhood was. That's a hard line I will not cross."

"O-Oh... b-but..."

The paw tightened around his crotch.

"But what?"

"I... I can't... I already..."

"Sounds like a 'you' problem," Sam muttered, with a smirk, enjoying immensely the power he was developing over the big bear.

"I... I want... You're asking me a lot..."

"I know. You want me? You have to play by the rules."

Roy's face scrunched up into a scowl, and there was a thrill of fear in Sam's stomach that made him smile and tighten his grip.

"I... I have... a rule too," said Roy, breathing as Sam began to stroke through his khakis.

"Oh? Finally growing a spine, are you?"

Sam was hardly listening. He leaned towards Roy, slipping his fingers past the waistband of the bear's pants. The bear was already rock hard, and every touch of fur on skin made Roy gasp and clench his jaw.

However, before Sam could begin unzipping those khaki pants, Roy reached down and grabbed his wrist. Sam gasped, his hand immediately pulling away from the man's cock, and soon the rabbit was face to face with a wide-eyed, angry bear.

"I have one rule," said Roy in a harsh whisper. It hardly seemed like the same Roy who was only a few minutes before happily bowling. "When I'm in town, I'm the only one."

"Wh-What?" said Sam, blinking his eyes, "What did I just say? I don't want anything serious with..."

"It's not serious. Every time in between you can do whatever you want," hissed Roy, "but when I dock, and I text, I'm who you go with."

Sam shuddered as the bear's paw tightened around his thin wrist. If he wanted to, he could have squeezed hard enough to break a bone, Sam had no doubt.

"You don't... you don't own me," muttered Sam, "You can't stop me from doing what I want. We're doing this because you can't get enough of me. Any time at all I can walk away. Forget I ever met you. Call the cops if you start to get creepy."

"But you won't. You could have done that before, when

you ran away," said Roy. "You want me, just like I want you."

"Don't... Don't get too full of yourself."

"But I'm right, aren't I?" asked Roy, before he pressed his face close to Sam's muzzle. The rabbit could smell the beer on his breath. "You gave me three rules. I gave you one. That's fair, isn't it?"

"Big rule..."

"About as big as your rules," said Roy. "So?"

"Let go of my wrist," Sam said, making his voice calm.

At once, obediently, Roy let go, and ceded power back to Sam. Regardless, he waited for a definitive answer, leaning forward on his seat. Sam blinked his eyes and rubbed his aching wrist. Exclusivity one night every two months? Maybe he could do that. He smiled, slowly, letting the sides of his muzzle curl up, and nodded.

"You came pretty close to hurting me," said Sam, teasing the bear, "If it leaves a bruise I'm counting it as a hit, you understand? Unless, of course, I asked for it."

"Yes, Sam."

"Alright. Fine, have it your way," said Sam. "I can live with that. One day every couple months, I am all yours... and you're all mine."

With that, Sam reached down once again and, with dexterous fingers, unbuttoned the man's trousers and pulled down the zipper. At once he felt the man's cock through his boxers, and soon pulled it roughly through the hole in the front. Roy gasped as he was exposed, and he desperately looked around the bowling alley. However, there was no one there.

"S-Sam?"

"Like I said, good boys get a treat," muttered the rabbit before he began to slowly jack his paw up and down the bear's length. Roy gasped, leaning forward, but that pinned Sam's hand under his fat, and Sam had to push Roy to sit back and give the rabbit room to work.

Huffing and struggling not to groan, Roy reached up to bite his paw as Sam stroked him. All the while, the rabbit was staring directly into his face, smile wide. Roy breathed in deeply.

"I... l-love... your teeth."

Sam's face fell in confusion at this strange thing to say and tilted his head, making his lop ears hang funny, and making Roy smile. He put one finger in front of his mouth and wiggled it.

"You... You have buck teeth. It's... c-cute... ah!"

The pace of the strokes increased as Sam's smile grew more malicious. His paw tightened and picked up speed, and Roy's cock was enveloped in a soft, tight tunnel that he began to hump into.

"Yeah, real cute," Sam whispered into his ear as he pulled on it with his other hand. "Make more noises like that and the guy at the counter will hear you. You'll be in trouble, whipping your cock out in the middle of a place like this. Kids play here, you fucking pervert."

"A-ah..." he began to say, trying to answer, but he covered his mouth and concentrated on staying quiet.

"Maybe I'll call him over," whispered Sam. "He was, what? Maybe thirty? Bored out of his skull? Cute too. I bet his cock would make you scream."

"I... I'd like that..."

"Oh? And what happened to me being all yours and you being all mine?"

A hard, painful stroke made Roy moan around his mouth.

"I... I mean... you get to do whatever you want with me," Roy whispered, his voice growing high pitched and desperate. "If y-you wanted to..."

"Shop you around like a piece of meat?" whispered Sam. He was pressing his body up against Roy's, partially to cover up what he was doing, and partially just to feel more of the massive body completely under his control. "What if I wanted to toss you into a room blindfolded and let whoever was in there have their way with you? What then?"

"W-Would you be there?"

"Maybe," he said, his stroking becoming gentler, but no less fast. A treat for the good boy for playing along.

"Th-then y-yes... Yes... oh god..." he whispered, his jaw dropping. A little line of drool began to flow from the corner of his mouth. "S-Sam I'm... I'm close. P-Please?"

"If you cum now, I own you," whispered Sam, harshly, "Our rules start now."

"Y-Yes... Yes! Yes!"

Sam winced. That was a little loud. Despite his dirty talk, he didn't actually want that greasy-looking loser to come over here. He roughly squeezed Roy's cock.

"Quiet," he hissed.

"Y-Yes, yes, Sam."

"You want to cum? You want me to own you? Your last load as a free man?"

"P-Please, yes," Roy whispered, not wanting to be punished for speaking too loud again. He was just on the edge, desperate to cum. He was shaking.

"Alright then," said Sam, looking over the massive body of the bear that was, for the moment, completely under his spell. He resumed his gentle, fast strokes, paying close attention to the head to overstimulate the man, and Roy's breathing grew harsh and uneven.

"S-S-Sam..." he pleaded. "Saaam..."

"Cum, then, trash," Sam whispered, and his pace picked up, stroking the man fast and hard. Roy couldn't help but moan and he tried to stifle it with his paw, but still it came out, muffled but not muted.

At once, the bear's cock pulsed, and the tip began to explode with white cum which shot out several feet in front of that orange plastic chair and landed on the shiny hardwood floor of the bowling alley. Another throb, and another shot of cum escaped, and Roy, unable to stop himself from crying out, turned to bury his face in Sam's neck. However, as he did a third, weaker, stream of cum shot out, and from the change in trajectory, landed mostly on the sleeve of Sam's windbreaker.

Roy continued to try to muffle his scream using the soft fur at Sam's neck and managed to mostly keep himself from making too much noise as cum continued to dribble out. Sam pulled his paw away, discovering the mess on his sleeve, and he grimaced before looking down at Roy's cock where a wet, musky-smelling spot was pooling at the front of the bear's khakis. The sight made Sam smile, before he raised his sleeve towards the bear.

"You made a mess," he said, simply "Clean it up."

Sam grunted in surprise as the bear grabbed hold of his arm and pulled it eagerly towards his face. The rabbit was taken off guard by the bear's enthusiasm in licking his own cum off Sam's sleeve, and Sam blinked hard as he watched the show. The bear's tongue was long, and ran up and down the shiny polyester, licking up the mess and eagerly swallowing it, leaving spots behind in his beard. Then, he pulled the rabbit's sleeve down, and he began to kiss and suck the white fur of Sam's thin wrist, forgetting the mess entirely and using this as an excuse to simply lick and suck the man's furry wrist and paws. Sam let him and glanced over at the floor.

Roy's cum sat there, and Sam, drunk with power over the large man, smiled at the possibilities. Watching the bear lick his own mess up off the floor, ass up, and utterly dominated in public, would have been a power trip, but Sam's better judgment caught up with him. The guy at the kiosk probably heard the lewd noises and likely saw the back of Roy's head as he furiously bathed Roy's arm. Plus, it was a different kind of power trip to just leave it for someone else to clean up.

"Zip up," said Sam, pulling his arm away from Roy. The bear, not done in the slightest, whined a little. Sam reached over with the arm slick with saliva and picked up his beer, taking a long draught of it as he watched Roy stuff himself back into his underwear, zip up his khakis, and button his fly. Sam smirked at the wet spots on Roy's lap. It would be obvious what happened. Roy would be banned from another place. Sam smiled, enjoying the power that this bear had simply handed to him.

Once Roy was somewhat presentable, Sam then pushed the bear's beer back into his paw, let him take one more long drink, and then grabbed his wrist and started to lead him away from the lane.

"B-But..." muttered a groggy Roy, "what about the game?"

"Fuck the game," said Sam, and that was all it took. He led the bear to the entrance of the bowling alley, where the man at the kiosk was giving them both an odd look. They dropped off their rented bowling shoes in exchange for their street shoes. Sam stood tall and confident, and Roy was a disheveled mess.

No more words were needed. As soon as their street shoes were back on their feet, Sam led Roy out the door. He had power over this man. Actual, real power. He could make Roy do anything, and the lovesick fool would do it.

As they exited the alley, Sam let go of Roy's wrist temporarily, just to light up a cigarette, before he took him by the wrist again.

"So, Roy," said Sam, blowing out a cloud of smoke directly into Roy's face, "you ever give anyone a tour of your ship?"

The airlock hissed as it closed, and immediately Sam and Roy were entangled with one another. The freighter was a one-seat-er, but that one seat had a little give on either side. It was dark in there, except for that little pilot light above them. It was tight and cramped, with hardly enough room for the two of them to start taking off their clothes, but they managed it. Soon Roy had pressed his back against the wall opposite the airlock, his ass up on one of the consoles, while Sam sat in the driver's seat sideways, cock jutting straight up as he poured lube over it.

Roy watched him, blinking his eyes. Unlike the other times, he wasn't pulling out a condom. A little anxiety came over the bear's chest as he realized that Sam was stroking himself hard without it, and then went up on his knees to lay his head between Roy's fat tits.

"A-Aren't you... going to use a rubber?"

"No," said Sam, and that smile dared him to object.

Roy's eyes widened. Sam had a lot more sex with random strangers than Roy did. It was dangerous. Stupid even. He could have insisted. He could have said no. Instead, he leaned back, bracing his arms against the consoles and ceiling, and pushed his feet up against the opposite wall formed by the airlock. He was accordioned up, and he knew he would cramp up if they stayed like this too long, but Sam was in charge. Sam was in control.

The rabbit grabbed hold of the bear's fat thighs for lever-age and soon guided his slick cock to the huge man's hole. It was intoxicating, seeing how much bigger the man was com-pared to him. Sam couldn't help but giggle, before he uncere-moniously pressed his cock into the tight hole.

"Fuck!" cried Roy, "Ah! St-Stop! Stop!"

"What's the matter? First time?" taunted Sam, knowing very well it was. "Never even tried a finger down there?"

"C-Couldn't... I couldn't reach."

"Well, remember to breathe baby," said Sam. "I got something for you."

"H-Huh?" asked Roy, before he took the man's advice, breathing deeply in and out as he felt that insistent cock starting to push into his hole. His breathing grew ragged. It stung so much. For a moment he worried that this is what he had done to Sam – what he still wanted to do to Sam. How could anyone like this?

Still, he breathed in deeply, with eyes closed, but as he did, he suddenly got a whiff of something harsh and chemical that made him cough. Roy's eyes shot open, and he saw that Sam was holding a small bottle up to his nose, making him breathe that burning odor in.

"Breathe, baby," said Sam, before he too brought the popper to his own nose and gave a deep sniff before capping it.

Roy's coughing ceased, leaving behind a strange warmth in his chest and forehead, and a giddy sort of feeling in his brain. The fog made him blink hard, pressing his head back against the wall. He groaned.

After several seconds, Sam said, "That's it. That's what I wanted," before he began to push back into Roy's ass.

Roy cried out anew, his jaw hanging open as he called out. He knew he didn't have to be quiet, the cabins were soundproof as well as airtight after all. There was almost no resistance as Sam slipped into his hole, and Roy found that for several seconds he couldn't even clench down there. He groaned in pain as Sam hissed in pleasure, and the bear felt the bunny's hands tighten around the flab on either side of his belly.

"Nothing beats a fat ass," muttered Sam, before he looked up into Roy's face, "How do you feel?"

How did he feel? Good, strangely. That bottle he'd sniffed had left behind a giddy feeling, and he felt happy to let Sam take him. Even his legs weren't complaining from how they were bent, and he felt his whole body relaxing against the console he was sitting on.

"G-Good."

It was a brief feeling, however, as Sam pulled out his cock without warning and mercilessly drove it back in. Roy cried out, feeling as if he should tense up, but finding he was unable. He was relaxed, whether he liked it or not, and it was lucky that when it came to Sam, he liked it. The rabbit picked up his pace at once, muttering a sudden string of profanity as his cock pistoned in and out of the heavy bear's entrance.

The pain was lessened with the drug relaxing him, and each thrust of the rabbit's cock against his inner walls was turning into an electric pleasure that emanated from deep inside. It seemed to push up through him, buzzing against his cock, and making it rise up, aching slightly from cumming so recently.

"Yeah, fuck," grunted Sam, before he buried his face in Roy's chest and belly, kissing and licking the fur there. He sniffed the musk coming off the bear's horny body, his lips curled, and his eyes closed in deep concentration as he fucked up into the other man's fat ass. The sight of Roy licking the cum from his arm was fresh in his mind. He could make him do whatever he wanted. Whatever he wanted.

"Gonna…" muttered Sam between thrusts. His words were slurring as he too enjoyed the euphoric sensation of the relaxing chemicals. "Gonna buy you a leash. Keep you as a pet. God, you'd look good sleeping on the floor, eating my ass."

Roy shuddered. The effects of the drug were already wearing off, and the tightness and anxiety were returning. However, that meant that the pleasure was increasing as well, and his cock grew harder at the thoughts Sam was giving him.

"You'd like that. Quit your fucking job, live in my house, fuck you whenever I wanted."

"Y-Yes… please…"

"Fuck… Fuck me whenever I wanted," he continued, "Oh,

yeah, you're just a… dumb fucking animal when it comes to me, huh? Hole to breed or cock to suck, you don't care, as long as I told you so."

"Y-Yes!" Roy cried out, and he could feel himself getting close again. He reached down to touch his cock, but Sam slapped his paw away hard.

"You had your turn, big boy," said Sam, smiling, "Now it's my turn."

With that, he picked up the pace, not caring at all for Roy's pleasure as he fucked up into the freighter. The tight feeling around his cock made him groan and bury his face further in the soft folds of Roy's body. Underneath those folds, however, Sam could feel the power within. He wasn't just fat. He was a freighter. He lifted heavy boxes and hauled them onto his truck. He had a strong core, tight muscles in his arms, and everything covered by a layer of fat. Having someone this powerful – someone who could snap Sam's neck in seconds if he wanted to – begging for his cock was something Sam could not get enough of.

"Fuck!" he said, thrusting in and out, "You're… You're mine."

"Yes!" cried Roy.

Sam's voice cracked, and he closed his eyes, throwing his arms around the bear's belly and squeezing it as hard as he could as he thrust. Then, with a scream, he went over the edge, pounding hard into the man's eager ass and releasing his load deep inside. Sam pressed his forehead into Roy's tits and, with nothing else he could do to ride out the pleasure, he opened his mouth and bit down hard on Roy's nipple, causing the bear to scream in pain and surprise, before he too shot a weak stream of cum between them. Both were growling, reduced to snarling animals, trapped in that too-small space. Sam's last few thrusts were fast and hard, trying to fuck as much of himself into the bear as he could.

But it couldn't last forever. Sam's legs began to feel the exertion, and Roy grunted as he felt a tight, hot pain shoot up one of his legs. He whimpered, pulling away from Sam as he desperately tried to turn to sit down and put his leg on the floor in a more natural position as he massaged it. Sam let him, all of his attitude melted away with the white hot orgasm that was shooting through him. As Roy turned to sit normally in the cockpit of the freighter, Sam crawled up into the bear's lap – as there wasn't much room for him to be anywhere else. He rested his exhausted body against Roy's, and the two of them basked in the afterglow.

Sam wasn't thinking. He was lightheaded from the bear's musk, the aftereffects of the popper, and the afterglow of his orgasm, and in that moment of weakness, he turned his face towards Roy's and kissed him deeply, thrusting his tongue into the bear's muzzle. The bear wasted no time returning the kiss, his own long tongue spreading out inside the rabbit's mouth, nearly choking him, but making him shiver as well. Sam thought he would never forget how much bigger and stronger his new pet was, and as he ran his own tongue over those sharp fangs, he shivered anew.

Breathing hard, Sam laid his head against Roy's chest, and Roy encircled the rabbit in a hug, pressing him into his belly. Sam felt... nice. It was strangely cozy here, inside this tiny space, with a great big pillow of a man to rest against. He wanted to sleep. He wished he had simply invited the man back to the hotel room so they could. But then he realized with a smile that it was only around eleven at night outside. Roy didn't usually go to sleep until at least one or two, and that meant they had a few hours still to eat, and rest, and, maybe, mess around some more – or fuck again if they could manage it.

Roy, for his part, said nothing. His jaw was clenched shut

as he hugged the rabbit against his thick frame. The forbidden words were bubbling up. I love you. I love you. He held them instead in his mind. What else could this feeling be? This pleasant, euphoric bliss that he had only ever experienced after encountering Sam. It didn't matter to Roy that this was the fourth time the two men had ever met. It didn't matter that after today Roy would not see his rabbit for two more months.

For a moment, the two of them stayed that way, their breathing in sync and truly, deeply, madly happy. No barriers. No guard up. Nothing getting in the way of the tenderness that arose from everything they did to one another. They would never be happier than they were in that moment, holding one another in the cab of Roy's company freighter, as the plastic wrestlers watched with molded angry faces.

FIFTH ENCOUNTER:
HOUSE CALL

Sam. I'm getting in around midnight today.

Where do you want to meet?

Hello?

Hello?

Sam?
Unread, sent 11:49pm

Roy sat, staring at the light in the window. The neighborhood was nice, one of the inner districts of Seb Station that he thought he would never visit. Unlike the featureless aluminum-sided apartment blocks and utilitarian facades of the businesses in the dockside industrial park and neighborhood, this place seemed almost like it was planetside. Trees and bushes lined the boulevard, the pavement was real asphalt, and the houses and apartments here were constructed of real housing materials – brick, shingles, stucco, and cement. The false night sky was brighter here, and the ceiling screens illuminated the streets with a gorgeous view of Jupiter and the nearest of the numerous moons held in perpendicular orbit to Sebastian, looming massive in the sky.

The hover was a rental. It wouldn't have been feasible for Roy to get a rideshare here. He wasn't even sure he wanted to bother, and getting dropped off and abandoned by a cab in the middle of the nicest neighborhood in Seb seemed like a one-way ticket to the station brig. Then again, sitting parked in the street outside of a nice-looking house in a black hover watching the windows probably didn't endear him to the neighbors either.

Still, he stared and waited. His tablet sat on the dash, painfully quiet. Every so often his pawpad would swipe across the screen just in case he missed a call or text, and every time he would see that same message.

Sam?
Unread, sent 11:49pm

He grunted, looking back at the house. He wasn't even sure this was the right place. It was so nice. Sam was fancy, yes, with his suits and ties and nice shoes, but at the same time, he spent all his time in the neighborhood around the docks. That was a rough part of town, Roy realized, likely the worst part of the station. If he lived somewhere so nice, why did he go all the way down to the Riff-Raff or Fabula Galaxy, or eat at the Waffle Station, or meet with Roy at the Lucky Bowl? He could have been going to nice bars and nice restaurants.

Roy felt filthy. He had parked the freighter, wandered to the company offices just off the docks, and asked about Sam. Import-Export. That meant he had close ties with The Company. Richie in the office confirmed Samuel Thorn lived up in the inner burb of Seb Station. Then Roy simply typed the neighborhood into a search, along with Sam's phone number, and got a hit – a nice-looking house in the middle of the neighborhood.

The bear made his way to the hover rental booth, beeped his card to pay too much for a day of use, and didn't think as he drove the convoluted path up to this house in this neighborhood. He didn't think as he cut the engine, stared up into those windows, and waited.

We had a deal, Roy finally thought, eyes widening.

An hour passed, and as he waited, the last time he saw Sam played through his mind. The bowling alley, the taste of the beers, the conversation, the fascination they had with one another. Sam's hand around his cock, Sam's cock tearing open his ass, the euphoria of the popper, and the bliss of simply holding the rabbit. Dinner. The soft bed of the hotel. The hot shower in the morning. The goodbye that was, for once, friendly and excited for the next time.

As he thought longer about the encounter, he could feel himself growing hard. He grunted, looking away from the house and leaning his forehead against the steering column. What had he done wrong? It seemed so good. Why didn't he respond? Why isn't he checking his phone? Did something happen? Maybe he should go up and knock. Roy growled in frustration. If he knocked, and Sam was there and deliberately ignoring him, then what? What would he do? *What would he do?*

His paw reached down and rubbed his hardening cock through his trousers. His own pawpads and coarse fur couldn't compare to Sam's soft hands. In the cabin of his freighter, he had been growing more and more frustrated with just masturbating. He wanted to fuck Sam this time. He wanted to feel the rabbit's mouth around him. He wanted to fill that rabbit with his cum and watch him squirm and press down on him with his belly.

His frustration turned the fantasy violent then, as he imagined Sam struggling to breathe under Roy's mass, with the bear's cock still in his ass, eyes wide and gasping for breath as Roy imagined his body crushing and killing the rabbit. His paw began to unzip his jumpsuit before he started to reach down inside, taking his cock in his paw as well as he could around his bulk and through the fabric of his underwear. His breathing grew hard and fast as he lightly stroked himself, venting his frustration with dark fantasies of watching the rabbit suffer for breaking their rules so soon after they had made them.

He gasped as his fantasies were interrupted by a shattering noise, and a sudden dark liquid splashed on the windshield. He sat up, blinking, and saw the shards of a mug gathering at the base of the windshield, before he looked around for who had thrown a full mug of coffee at him.

Muffled by the closed door and window of the hover, Sam stood, rage on his face as he screamed, "What the fuck are you doing here?"

Elation came over Roy. *Him!* He sat back and smiled, despite Sam's harsh words. He then saw Sam's eyes traveling down his body, a look of mounting disgust on his face. Roy looked down himself and saw his jumpsuit unzipped to the crotch and the head of his hard cock peeking over the waistband. Roy hurried to stuff himself back into his clothes, but Sam's rage was white hot.

The rabbit was wearing striped pajamas, a silk robe, and house slippers, and so there was no sound when he kicked the side of the hover as hard as he could. Roy, needing to explain, opened the driver's side door and stood up.

"Sam!" he said.

"Get back in the car Roy!" Sam screamed, "Get back in

and fucking go!"

"I thought... you didn't answer your texts. I thought you..."

"What? You thought that was permission to fucking jack off in front of my house?" he demanded, "How did you even find...?"

"I... I searched for it. I put your number into a net search and this address was attached to it and I got the neighborhood from The Company and..."

"Fucking hell," said Sam, eyes wide in horror. Roy didn't bother to close the door to the hover as he ran around it, approaching the rabbit, but the rabbit stepped backwards, raising his arms, "Get the fuck away from me."

"I... I was worried."

Sam's mounting horror and panic was rubbing off on Roy, and he soon found himself fidgeting and panicking as well. He wanted Sam to be quiet. He was going to wake up the neighbors. He was going to call the police. Roy knew he needed to run away. He needed to jump back in the hover and go back to the docks. It was over. He knew he fucked up.

However, when someone else appeared at the door to Sam's house, Roy perked up, and then his eyes went wide.

She was probably around thirty, a wolf who was hastily buttoning up a blouse as she peered out the front door to see what was going on. Her figure was curvy, and if she wasn't terrified of the raving lunatic in front of Sam's house, she would have probably been pretty. Her eyes were wide at the sight of the huge bear and cowered as soon as Roy spotted her.

Roy's eyes went wide.

"Who's that?" asked the bear, his voice growing dark.

"Fucking leave," Sam insisted, ignoring the question, "I don't fucking want you here! Goddamn it, Roy, just fucking..."

However, before he could finish his sentence, he was jostled when Roy snatched up the collar of his robe. Instantly, Sam went silent, his eyes wide in terror at the huge man pulling him close. Roy's eyes were suddenly wild. Gone was the timid urge to explain himself. Gone was the soft, pathetic man routine. Roy was pissed, and the rabbit felt an ancient animal urge to run away and hide. Instead, he was pulled in until their muzzles were inches apart, and froze.

"You knew," Roy hissed, "You knew I was getting in soon."

"R-Roy…"

"Who is that? Why is she…?"

"None of your fucking busin…"

"You are mine!" Roy roared, shaking the rabbit, "And I'm yours! Those are the *rules*. That was the promise. One day! That's all either of us asked for. One day! I do whatever you want, and you don't fuck around!"

"God… I… Oh god…" Sam stammered, frightened out of his mind by the rage-filled bear. Even the appearance of tears streaming down the bear's face didn't lessen his terror.

"You brought her here but not me?" Roy said, before he repeated in a massive roar, "*Not me!?*"

The woman screamed, and that high pitched sound seemed to knock Roy out of his blind rage. Suddenly, he let go of Sam, who immediately stumbled backwards, eyes wide. He slowly began taking steps backward as the bear, wracked with sudden sobs and growls, stepped away, leaning against the hover as he covered his face with his paws.

Lights in windows throughout the neighborhood flicked on, and Sam was suddenly self-conscious. *The HOA is going to love this*, he thought, in a moment of surprising lucidity.

"The…" stammered Roy, who seemed to be wilting under the attention of all the house lights turning on, "The d-diner… I'm going to… to eat…"

"Roy…" muttered Sam, but he wasn't sure what he was

even going to say. Cuss him out? Comfort him? He stood, dumb for a moment, as he waited for Roy to say more.

"Be there," said Roy, peering at Sam through his fingers. Those eyes were wet and bloodshot, but there was something else there. A threat. Sam, with a thrill of fear, realized that Roy knew where he lived now. Any time he wanted, he could come over. Sam felt like he wanted to vomit as the bear turned, climbing back into the hover and slamming the door shut, before the engine spun up and it sped away down the street.

Sam stood for a moment, his heart pounding as he watched Roy go. This wasn't fun anymore. What the hell was that?

"S-Sam?" said the wolf at the door, Kay. Sam had nearly forgotten about her. He forced a laugh, reaching up to adjust his ears, and he shrugged.

"Some rando from the docks," he joked, "probably pissed about how slow the asteroid belt's getting cleared. I know I'd rather all these fucking trucker losers stop showing up here."

He walked back up to the front door and glanced behind him. Some of the lights in his neighbors' houses were turning back off, but some stayed on. He felt like he was being watched. His hackles raised. First one kind of stalking and then another. He put on a brave face for Kay and walked up to the door.

"Go back inside, baby. We can keep on…"

"I… I think I want to go home, Mr. Thorn," she said.

Mister. Sam frowned. He had been Daddy not five minutes ago, but he's suddenly *mister?* He watched as Kay walked into the living room, grabbed her purse, adjusted her blouse and started to leave.

"H-Hey! Kay. It's alright. He left!"

"That's… I mean… I'm just not in the mood anymore," she said, shaky all of a sudden. "Goodnight. M-Maybe another time."

The woman walked across the lawn towards her own hover parked discreetly down the street. Sam, still in his pajamas, rushed after her.

"Kay!" he cried, "C'mon! After that nice dinner? Are we going to just let one asshole ruin our whole night?"

However, she ignored him. She pulled her keys out of her purse and pressed the door's unlock button. Sam bristled anew as he heard the beep and rushed after her.

"Kay, stop."

He reached over to grab her wrist, but she pulled it away, looking at him with a sudden anger.

"I'm going home, Sam," she said, "Thanks for dinner. Goodnight."

"You can't fucking..." he said, before he caught himself as she winced at him swearing at her just like he swore at Roy. "Come on! The night is still young! At least finish your drink; you're shaking."

She didn't answer. Instead, she climbed into her hover and started to close the door. Sam felt the urge to try to grab the door before it closed to keep her here. He had been working Kay all night, breaking down her defenses. They met at that company retreat last week, and he had spent all week buttering her up. It was all about to be for nothing.

However, the lingering lights in the neighboring houses caught his attention. He clenched his jaw and, under the judgment of his neighbors, he let the hovercar's door shut. Kay's engine turned on, and soon the hover started to drive away. Sam stared at it go, brow furrowed.

That fucking bear.

He restrained his urge to scream. He turned away from the road, made his way back to his house, and entered, slamming the door shut behind him. Even then, he did not scream, as he realized what Roy had said.

Be there.

Terror came over Sam as he slowly slid down his front door, falling into a terrified crouch. What had he done? What the fuck was Roy doing here? Roy had mentioned something about messages. Where was his tablet?

He groaned, his knees complaining as he stood up on his feet before he started to head upstairs. He rushed into his bedroom and, sure enough, there was his tablet. He hadn't brought it on his date with Kay – young people were such Luddites when it came to tech and texting culture from when Sam was a kid, so he tried to keep it under wraps – and he picked up the tablet. Sure enough, there were five missed calls, and a series of unread texts.

Getting in around midnight today. It was already around 1:30. Roy had to have been waiting out there for at least an hour.

Of course. The last time was two months ago. Every two months, the bear came around. Last time was good, yeah, and he had been looking forward to it for a while, but… two months was a long time. Sam had forgotten. He was so preoccupied with sleeping with a nice girl for once that he'd forgotten all about Roy, and now…?

The bear was going to kill him. Sam somehow knew Roy wanted him dead. If he went to the diner, he might die. If he didn't go, Roy would drive back up here later tonight, break into his house, and he would die for sure. Sam's eyes widened as he reached up to clutch the sides of his head. He'd fucked up. He poked the bear, so to speak, and now it was catching up to him. He remembered all at once all that stuff he had said to Roy last time at the bowling alley. How seriously had the bear taken it? Surely the bear didn't actually think…

But of course, Sam wasn't that stupid. He knew exactly what he had been doing. Roy had believed it, every word, in all sincerity, and here Sam was having a little fun, and now he was on the hook for everything he had agreed to two months ago.

He barely remembered his own words – he'd been so caught up in the power he had over the bear, that he had just babbled on, and when Roy had countered with his own rule, he let it slide.

He imagined what was going to happen to him as he sat on the bed. He imagined himself strangled to death in the alley behind the Waffle Station. He imagined his own busted down front door, and someone finding his body in the morning stuffed in the garbage outside. He imagined Roy standing over him, reaching for him. He imagined those big paws around his neck.

He reached down, cupping his hardening cock. His eyes were wide, and he was terrified, but somewhere, deep down, he knew that there had been rules, clearly set out, and he had broken them. The sight of Roy in his mind's eyes, immense, cast in shadow, and out for his blood, made blood rush to Sam's cock. It was the pill. It must have been the pill. He'd discreetly taken his little blue pill with dinner so he could perform for Kay, but now it was affecting him.

He reached inside his pajama pants, remembering that very first night with Roy. That awkward, painful fuck in that cramped apartment. He remembered that massive weight pressing down on his chest. The feeling of being unable to breathe, being unable to control what was happening. He remembered the edge of pain, and imagined what it would be like for it to have gone further, to press down harder on him, until he broke.

His breathing grew shallow and his eyes continued to widen, staring off into the middle distance as he continued to imagine Roy and that chest-rumbling roar that he had blasted into the rabbit's face.

"What the fuck," he said, realizing that he was masturbating to Roy murdering him. Roy was jealous; dangerously jealous. He was legitimately dangerous. Sam should be calling the police to report this, but... instead, he gripped his cock and stroked up and down, leaning back on his bed as he moaned.

Pleasure ripped through him and he squirmed while stroking his cock. What would he do? Beat him? Bite out his throat? Rape him? He breathed harder, stroking faster. He reached up a paw to his mouth and bit down as hard as he could, feeling the pain in his paw and imagining Roy doing the same. Sam remembered him licking his entire arm clean and imagining if he had gone further driving those sharp teeth into his wrist as he plowed Sam, tearing him apart, and all the while telling him exactly what he did wrong.

Mine.

Mine.

You are mine.

He gasped, his cock twitching as he felt the flood of pleasure intensify. His toes curled and uncurled as they hung off the bed, and he thrust his hips up off the mattress. Cum erupted from his cock, and he whined Roy's name as he did, finally remembering that moment in the freighter cab, when the bear had held him so gently. If he was dead, would Roy still hold him like that? How long? Until the cops came to carry him away? Until Sam was buried in the ground? If they never caught him, would Roy show up at his funeral? Would he cry? Would he leave flowers at Sam's grave?

He tensed, cum dribbling onto his pajama shirt.

He loves me, he thought, *And I'm going to die.*

A moment later, as the afterglow wore off, he blinked his eyes and clenched his jaw. *That was stupid.* He lay back, arms up above his head, coming down from the euphoric high of masturbation. Did that accomplish anything? No. Did he feel better about a jealous stalker on the loose? Also no.

He swallowed, staring at his ceiling. He had to finish this.

One way or another this had to stop. He'd taken it too far. He'd let Roy in too much. He'd let the bear fall in love with him, and now...?

Do I love...?

He stopped the thought before it could form by sitting up and starting to unbutton his pajamas. He tossed the sullied shirt into the laundry hamper and put the silk robe over the bed before he glanced at his tablet. He had to say something. Do something.

Slowly, his hand hovered over the emergency contact button in his phone app. Three taps and the cops would be on the line. He could send them after Roy at the Waffle Station. They would take him in, bring him down to the brig, he would lose his job and just... leave. Be gone from Sam's life. That would be it. Three taps away from never having to think about Roy ever again.

However, he froze, and slowly his fingers began to tap elsewhere. He opened up the messenger app, and he stared at Roy's last text.

Sam?
Sent 11:49pm

Sam stared at his own name and, somehow, though those three letters and a question mark, he could sense the bear's feelings. The frustration. The disappointment.

That doesn't excuse him fucking stalking me, but...

Sam typed out a message, hating himself as he did. Every few taps, he felt the urge to delete it and go back to the emergency number, but every time something within made him ignore it, until finally he hit send.

Be there in 20 min

Unread, sent 1:43pm

Then, as Sam watched, he saw a change come over the text. Underneath, the unread notification changed.

Be there in 20 min
Read

Too late to take it back now. Sam slipped off his pajama pants and slippers. He was still wearing his compression socks and girdle – he had been planning on keeping the shirt on while fucking Kay after all – and so he just changed back into a simple shirt and trousers. He wasn't looking to impress anybody now. He was going to end this, one way or another.

A notification noise from his tablet caused him to turn, and he quickly went to check it. He had to stifle a laugh at Roy's reply.

Ok 🐻🗡️

This fucking bear, thought Sam with a smile as he slipped on a pair of loafers and grabbed his keys off the bedside table. It wasn't until he was halfway out the door that he remembered that that 'fucking bear' was in the process of ruining his life and made an effort to banish the smile from his face.

Roy sat in the Waffle Station. He had a fluffy waffle, a fried sausage patty, and two eggs over easy on his place, steaming, fresh, and looking delicious, but he just stared down at them. His eyes were red and wet still, and the waitress gave him a brief look of sympathy as she poured him a cup of black coffee.

The bear did not eat for a while and stared down at his food. He knew he had to eat. That was part of the job. Eat.

Sleep. Prepare yourself for another long, lonely stretch of space, with no one to talk to but yourself and the action figures on your console. To prepare yourself for another long stretch of space where the only thing to amuse yourself is whatever you managed to bring along with you, and thoughts of *him*.

He leaned forward, resting his elbows on the table and pressing his paws into his face. What did he just do? He fucked up. Finally. This must have been the time that went too far. He shouldn't have gone there. He shouldn't have yelled at him. He shouldn't have grabbed him and shaken him around. He said he was on his way, but now… now he wasn't so sure he should. He considered picking up his tablet and texting back, telling Sam not to bother, and to agree to never see him again, but every time he did, the tablet seemed so heavy that he couldn't seem to pick it up out of his pocket.

A bell above the door rang. Someone came in. Roy did not look up. It was only when a white-furred paw entered his vision and stole the sausage from his plate that he looked up.

Sam stood, chewing on his sausage, eyes half-lidded and looking annoyed. He stood, looming over the big bear. He smelled intensely of cigarettes. It smelled like he'd smoked a whole pack on the way here to handle the stress. Eventually, the rabbit swallowed, cleared his throat and, without asking, sat down at the table across from Roy.

"If this goes on, one of us is gonna end up dead," muttered Sam.

Roy stared at him, frowning deeply. He blinked his eyes, before he clenched his jaw and nodded in agreement.

"I don't know what to do," he said, his voice low.

"Maybe start by not being so fucking intense," muttered Sam, before he gestured to the plate, "Eat."

"But…"

"Eat. You know The Company needs you alive and fed.

Hell, you probably have some of my stuff in that freighter of yours. I need you to drive out on time."

Slowly, Roy nodded, before he picked up his fork and began to cut into his waffle. He took a bite, not even bothering to put any syrup or butter on it. It tasted of vaguely sweet nothing.

"The girl…" muttered Roy, "I… thought you were gay."

Sam shrugged, "I swing both ways. I didn't divorce Mabel because she was a lady. I divorced her because she was a bitch."

"Oh."

"For your information, I've been trying to get with Kay for a week. I met her at my boss's penthouse suite during a work thing at the top of Seb. Y'know? The big dome thing on top?"

"People live there?"

"Like half a dozen people live there, each in their little fiefdom where they survey the little people toiling away below," muttered Sam with a little obvious disdain for his bosses. "Man-made lake up there, y'know? Instead of a swimming pool they built a whole fucking lake, with trees and grass, and sunshine you can turn off and on with a lightswitch any time of day that feels almost real."

"Wow…"

"Saw Kay there in a one-piece, looking fat and juicy, and I brought her a drink, and we hit it off. We met each other off and on the rest of the week, going out. Today I made her a home-cooked meal. Stroganoff, and some of mama's carrot cake for dessert. She loved it. Things were getting hot and heavy, I was about to go all the way and then…"

"You saw me…?"

Sam scowled, before he shook his head, "She saw you, staring up at the window. She thought you were peeping on her."

"I… I wasn't."

"No, you were peeping on me," muttered Sam, "with your

dick out no less."

"I'm… I'm s-sorr…"

"No, you don't get to just say *sorry* and then we try again. You're fucked up, Roy."

"But you broke the rules."

"Because I was seeing Kay tonight instead of you? I missed the text, alright? I was too busy preparing for tonight. I kept my phone on the charger all day."

"Still… it was two months ago. You had two months to get ready for me."

"I had two months to forget, you mean. Some of us have stuff going on in our lives in-between random hookups in the middle of the night!"

Sam's voice was rising, and a warning glance from the chicken waitress made him grimace and lower it.

"What I'm saying is maybe this whole thing was a bad idea," muttered Sam, "And maybe just a little bit it's… it's my fault. Maybe. I was going to call the cops on you, y'know. Have them pick you up here."

"I… I expected that."

"But I… I couldn't… I mean…" muttered Sam, trying to find a point in all his rambling, "I wanted to… y'know, give you a piece of my mind instead of just hauling you off. That is if you can be fucking cool for like two minutes."

"I… I can."

"Good," Sam grunted, before he leaned forward, frowning, and said, "Since you fucking insist on making this more than it needs to be, let's talk."

"We… We talked about it last time. You set your rules."

"Man, I was horny!" Sam muttered as he slumped over and rolled his eyes, "Half of the shit I said was to get a rise out of you, the other half I don't even fucking remember. I was laser focused back then on fucking you. Today, not so much. I am clear headed and not thinking with my dick, and I expect you to do the same, alright?"

As he spoke, a mug of black coffee was slammed in front of Sam, splashing a little on the table. He looked up to see the waitress staring down at him. She didn't say anything, but by the twitch of her comb and the set of her beak, it was clear she wasn't much a fan of Sam. She moved on a moment later and Sam cleared his throat.

"So?" said Sam.

"S-So what?"

"What do you want?" Sam said, sounding weary as he said it, "The rules are out the window. Hell, us fucking is probably out the window at this point, but still, I don't like loose ends, and I don't like getting fucking stalked, but neither do I like the idea of having to press charges on you and having everyone on Seb Station find out I go down to the gay bar at the docks to get my dick wet. So? What do you want?"

Roy paused. This was his chance to speak. It was clear what he wanted, but he just needed the courage and permission to say it. Finally free to speak, he sat up a little straighter.

"Why did you invite the girl to your house?" asked Roy.

"What?"

"You brought me to a hotel – or stayed in my room at the company apartment bloc. Your neighborhood's not that far from the docks. Why...?"

Sam seemed suddenly nervous. "Not your business. I don't want to track people like you back into my life."

"Oh."

"That's why I never wanted us to be serious," muttered Sam, shrugging. "Yeah, I bring girls home and wine and dine them with home-cooked meals, while I fuck faggots like you in bathroom stalls and in the backseats of cars. That's the kind of person I am. I have never, not even once, pretended I was some kind of saint. If you ever thought I was some beautiful, perfect queer angel, then that was on you for thinking that."

"I… I knew you weren't…"

"Then why go to my house? Why freak out when you found me with a woman? *What do you want from me?*"

"I love you!" cried Roy, suddenly, pounding both of his fists on the table. "That's what I want. I want… I want you to love me too."

Sam had to laugh, leaning back with one arm draped over his chair. "Are you fucking joking? You hardly know me. We have known each other a combined five days so far. Less than five days! We've known each other for a matter of fucking hours all put together. You don't fucking *love* me. You *can't possibly* love me."

"I… But I…"

"And even if you did, have you fucking met me?" demanded Sam, "You're a loser, fine, but I am no fucking catch. Falling in love with me was a bad idea for Mabel, and it's a bad idea for everyone else too. I am not looking for that. Never again."

"Then… Then we can go on like we were. One day every two months, like we planned."

Sam scoffed, "That plan fell through, and you were the one who decided not to be chill about it."

"Only because you were the one who broke the rules!"

"Who the fuck cares about *rules!?*" demanded Sam, suddenly leaning forward, "You're a fucking adult; act like it. You can do what you want and I can do what I want. We don't *belong* to one another. If you think you own me, you can fuck right off to hell, you understand me?"

"You… You may not have been serious in the bowling alley but… but I was," muttered Roy, "Every single word."

"Bully for you. Sucks to suck, Roy. Maybe that means you should heal your own damage before you come after me about mine, alright?"

"You don't know what it's like," muttered Roy, eyes widening. His voice was gentle. He was trying to get through to the rabbit. "Sitting there, surrounded by nothing and no one. Before I met you I was sure... I was sure I was going to go insane. Die in that cab like old Harold having a heart attack. I wondered if it would be better... better to just die."

Sam rolled his eyes, leaning back with his arms cross, but he said nothing.

"Then... Then you started paying attention to me. You were beautiful, and soft, and you made me excited. You were mean to me, but... but it was like I was in on it. Like you were mean to me *for me*. I... I liked it. I wanted more. Then... then you came and found me, and... and I thought maybe that meant that... that we could be more. Something more. You liked me enough to come find me. Nobody... nobody ever did that for me before. Nobody ever thought of me like that. Only you. Only... Only you. If that's not love..."

"It isn't," hissed Sam. "It is not fucking love, whatever it is. You're obsessed with me, Roy. That's it. You're insane and I think you need to get fucking help, but look for it elsewhere because *I am fucking done.*"

With that, Sam started to stand up to leave. However, the bear's paw shot out, gripping him hard around the wrist. Sam's eyes widened as he felt the harsh squeeze of the man's tight grip and clenched his jaw.

"Let go, Roy."

"I... I..." began Roy, trying to find something to say.

"Let go!"

Sam began to pull, grunting as the bear's tight grip held him in place. He reached up with his other hand then to try to pry the bear's finger's open, but Roy countered his movement, crushing his other hand in the bear's other massive paw. Roy pulled Sam closer, eyes wide, and tried to stammer out more words, trying to explain again, to explain what he loved about Sam, but unable to articulate it. He opened and closed his jaw as his paws grew tighter and tighter. Sam's own eyes widened as pain began to envelop his wrists.

"Cut that shit out!" cried a disinterested cook behind the counter. The chicken seemed poised to rush in and stop a fight as soon as it got out of hand.

Soon, Roy ran out of words, and pulled the struggling rabbit in close, to show him how much he loved him. He bent down, putting his muzzle awkwardly into the rabbit's face, forcing a kiss on him. Sam struggled, trying to shake his hands free, before he cocked back a leg and swung it up to strike the bear between the legs. Roy roared, his grip weakening, and Sam was able to pull one of his hands away and was preparing to pry himself out of Roy's grip.

Roy, frightened, disoriented, and in pain, felt his instincts take over. He stood up straight, tensed up, and cocked back a wrist. In the next moment, Sam felt a sharp pain, as Roy's fast fist cracked the rabbit across his face. The black and white rabbit was dazed, and his legs fell out from under him such that the only thing holding him up was the arm that Roy was holding.

"That's it!" screamed the chicken, running up with a heavy plastic tray, "Out! Fucking out!"

Roy tried to drag Sam away, working entirely on instinct. The rabbit was dazed and could hardly take a step. There was no more struggle for the moment. However, when that chicken ran up and gave Roy a crack upside the head with her tray, he roared and let go of Sam.

"Get out!" said the chicken, and immediately the entire rest of the Waffle Station was armed and ready. The hound dog cook with the cigarette hanging from his mouth had a knife.

The other waiters had their hands on chairs or glassware. Other customers seemed poised to start brawling. Roy, feeling the ache in his balls and the slight sting in his paw where he had struck Sam, stepped away from the rabbit, and then began to run.

Out into the night air, Roy fled until he finally found the rented hover he had parked outside. He climbed inside, turned it on, and began to speed off back towards the docks.

The only illumination in the hover as he pulled into the empty, lonesome lot was a single streetlamp that cast harsh shadows over everything. Roy cut the engine, sat back, and stared ahead into the darkness beyond the streetlight. During the short drive back to the rental place on the docks, he had been frantic, looking behind himself as if police were going to arrive any moment.

He had hit Sam. Hard. Sam had gone limp and fell to the floor.

Roy's eyes went wide, and he felt his vision blur. He could not stop the tears, even by suddenly closing his eyes and covering them with his paws.

He hit Sam. He could have killed him.

I'm never going to see him again.

The thought struck Roy and he immediately heard how stupid it was. He had more important things to worry about. He had just assaulted someone – twice. He needed to leave. He couldn't stay here. He knew he would get a talking to from his supervisors for skipping out on his allotted rest times, but he could always catch a nap in the freighter and get a meal from the vending machines before he pulled out. The important thing was leaving. He had some vacation time coming up. He never used any vacation time. Maybe he could use it, lie low for a while, take a break from the route, and let things at Seb

Station cool down.

That would mean it would be more than four months before he would roll through Sebastian Station again. That was
no great loss. It wasn't honestly anything more or less impres-
sive than any of the other stations and colonies on his route.

But Sam was here.

I'm never going to see him again.

His brow furrowed and a sob shot up from his chest. He
leaned forward, pressing his forehead against the steering column, and he growled, trying to calm down. He couldn't worry about that. He had to protect himself. Everyone in that
neighborhood had seen him. Sam had no reason not to press
charges. If he didn't leave...

He breathed in hard, trying to steel his expression, but only
succeeded in raggedly breathing in and coughing as the breath
hitched and got caught in his throat. He reached up with his
sleeves to rub the tears out of his eyes and leaned back in the
hover's driver seat. Calm. *Calm.* He had to forget about Sam.
He had to protect himself.

But even so, he couldn't. This had been his chance. He had
hardly been able to admit to himself exactly what he wanted from Sam. How could he admit it to the rabbit's face? He
didn't want to be alone anymore. More than loving Sam, more
than the sex, more than preventing himself from going insane,
he was tired of this life.

Sam asked him what he wanted, but it wasn't a matter of
want. It was a matter of *need*. He needed someone else to be in
his life, even if only for a few days out of the year. He needed
something to look forward to. He needed a distraction. He
needed someone to touch him. Good, bad, violent, or tender,
Sam represented more than just a companion to him. He represented something that Roy had been starved of his entire
life, and now that he had tasted it, he couldn't simply go back

to the darkness and loneliness.

But now it was over. He needed to stay away. Sam was right. One of them was going to end up dead at this rate. Roy opened the hover's door and stepped out, walking up to the kiosk he had parked in front of and pressing his card against the console. At once, the hover turned on by itself and drove into the parking lot, leaving Roy all alone in the streetlamp's light.

He pulled his tablet out of his pocket then. About 3:00. His freighter was sure to be loaded by now. If he pulled out now and got past the asteroid belt, he could sleep in the cabin for at least a few hours in transit, and he could bring along a sandwich to eat on the way. The Company only lightly admonished people who did things faster, as long as they didn't cause any damage to company property.

He started to walk towards the docks. When he got to the end of the line and turned around, he would put in for his vacation time. It would be good for him. No more getting cramped up in that tiny cabin. He could go back home, sleep in his own bed in his own apartment, eat planetside food for the first time in at least a year.

But his mind refused to give up on Sam. What about Sam? Roy knew what he should do. Ignore it. Try to move on. It was over. However, another, more animal part of him said the opposite.

Send a text. Apologize. Keep him in the loop.

He looked down at his screen and opened his messenger app. There he saw the last text he had sent, the ridiculous emojis that Sam had made fun of him for. He frowned, before he began to type, his fat fingers always making it slow going for him.

I'm pulling out early. Goodbye.

Unread, sent 3:03am

Roy stared at the text. Was that enough? He typed some more.

I'm sorry.
Unread, sent 3:07am

He began to approach the freighter docks, and held up his ID to open the gate, wandering like a zombie up to his freighter. As he suspected, the freight had been loaded, and he could leave any time. Just a visit to a vending machine and he would be ready. He turned towards a bank of machines, three soda machines and two half-stocked snack machines. There, he held up his card to the reader and chose four cans of soda, four bags of chips, two candy bars, and a large packet of jerky. He stuffed the snacks into his pocket to make a meal of it out in space, before he turned and walked on towards his freighter.

However, he could not stop himself from glancing down at his tablet. The message still sat unread. Maybe he was still recovering from the blow to his face.

With a wild impulse, he started to type again.

I'm taking vacation time. You won't see me in February.
Unread, sent 3:12am

He stood in front of the airlock of his freighter's cabin and stared at his tablet. Reception was hit or miss in open space. This was likely the last chance he would have to say… something. What? What could he have said?

He typed.

36 N Dublin st. Apt. B. Alba City. Planetside Mars.

Unread, sent 3:16am

His address. He almost didn't realize what he was doing until after he was halfway done typing, and even though he found it ridiculous, he kept it up. He was inviting Sam to his apartment.

If you want to see me again that's my place.
Unread, sent 3:19am

Pathetic. Absolutely pathetic. Roy growled, stuffing the tablet back into his pocket stuffed with snacks and froze in front of the airlock. He almost expected to see another business card there, just like last time, but there was none. Sam had truly abandoned him this time, and here he was, still trying desperately to keep the man on the hook.

He fished his tablet out again, unable to stand the suspense. Maybe there was more he had to say, or maybe he could delete the messages before they went through and Sam could read them. He opened the messenger app up once again and stared at the screen.

If you want to see me again that's my place.
Read

He froze. Sam was awake, and he had read the message. Roy waited for a moment, expecting the rabbit to start typing, or react, or send an emoji or something, but there was nothing. Roy frowned, his shoulders drooping. He held up his ID to the freighter's airlock and the door hissed open. He climbed inside, his eyelids drooping from the late hour, and he let the door close behind him. He knew then it was over once and for all. Sam had read the text and didn't fucking care.

One more word, and then Roy tossed the tablet to the ground, started up his engine, and began to pull out of Sebastian Station.

Goodbye.
Read

Sixth Encounter:
Bachelor Pad

CIGARETTE hanging from his mouth, Samuel stepped off the last shuttle of the day and with practiced movements, walked down the street towards the motel, intent on buying a room for the night in advance. He was in a retro mood that day, wearing a chunky leather jacket that filled out his shoulders and torso, butch work boots, and the skinniest jeans he could zip himself into. He felt good stepping out of the house that day, but now that he was down to the docks and he saw all the regulars hanging around on the way to Fabula dressed in outrageous colors and flowy robes and tassels, he felt suddenly out of place. He was trying to dress young that day, he knew, but people hadn't worn this silhouette for a couple decades at least.

He reached up to snatch the cigarette out of his mouth. No matter. He could ditch the jacket at the hotel before he left and go in tight jeans and the flannel button-up he wore underneath. Grungy, in a way that read very 'straight boy college student experimenting.' Then again, he wasn't a college student anymore. He was a grown-ass man.

He paid for the room in advance and began to walk down to the clubs. Fabula was hopping as usual, but for some reason he wasn't feeling it. Maybe it was him deflating from the realization about how he had dressed, but he didn't feel like hanging around a bunch of partying gay college kids, trying to pick off the ones that he could manipulate into coming to bed with him. That left the Riff-Raff, but even that, that didn't appeal either. He felt safe there at least – the owner didn't care if you were a fag as long as you paid your tab and didn't cause problems. Other bars sprang up every now and then, a few that he hadn't even tried yet, but he knew most of them would be dockside dives for the good-ole'-boy dockworkers or down-and-out pubs that were basically flophouses for transients unlucky enough to find themselves all the way out around Jupiter.

Paralyzed by indecision, Sam wandered around and around the five or six blocks that constituted the neighborhood immediately surrounding the docks, and even strayed out into the residential neighborhood next door in case something new had opened up, but there was nothing. Nothing interesting caught his eye. Maybe it was the uncomfortable tightness of his jeans, but he didn't really feel like sleeping around today.

He grimaced. He'd come all the way down here to slum it up but seems like he'd wasted his time. Nothing here interested him. The thought of making it with another barely legal exogeology major bored him – been there, done that – and even just the thought of bar food and vodka soda made him frown. He was three cigarettes deep into his walk before he finally turned down an alley and saw where his walk had been funneling him.

Waffle Station. Yeah. He was hungry. He could eat. He started walking towards it. It was almost time for the late night freights to get in after all. He smiled a little, and a face crossed his mind's eye.

He stopped, his smile fading.

Frozen to the spot, the only movement of his body was the mechanical movement of the cigarette between his fingers moving up to his muzzle and then dangling lazily to his side. He flicked the ashes onto the floor.

He won't be there either.

Sam realized something. When he came out here, he was searching. He usually was – a hot piece of ass or an evening talking to folks. An evening away from his life as a middle-manager and go-between for different branches of The Company. Maybe even just a bit of fun.

Now, he was searching for someone in particular. He hadn't even realized it until he saw the lights on in the Waffle Station window. Roy. He was looking for Roy.

He laughed, suddenly turning away from the diner, shaking his head. He couldn't face being in there right now. Instead, he walked back closer to the docks. Maybe this had been a mistake. Maybe he could just go home. It wasn't that late. It wasn't the time of night where the rideshares price gouged you for being desperate quite yet. Tonight was a bust. He would return to the hotel, get his deposit back, stop by the docks to get a ride home and…

And what? Why did it feel so different? Sam was frustrated as he dropped the butt of his cigarette to the ground and crushed it under his thick boots, before lighting up another one. He knew Roy wasn't here. Roy was taking time off from his route. His text said so. Sam reached up to touch his cheek where the bear had slapped the hell out of him. An evening in the hospital to make sure he didn't have a concussion, and he was right as rain. No lasting harm except a black eye that cleared up within a week.

Are you seriously considering seeing him again?

The voice was his own; a more rational part of his own mind. The one that had been warning him to stay the hell away from that psychopath since the very first day they met.

Sam, slowly, reached into his pocket and pulled out his tablet. Even though the kids weren't into people being glued to electronics these days, ever since missing that text he made sure he always had it with him. He opened it up, tapped the messenger app, and scrolled down past all the clients and business associates and coworkers until he found *him*.

36 N Dublin st. Apt. B. Alba City. Planetside Mars.

Insane. Absolutely insane. Sam pressed the power button on his tablet and stuffed it back into his pocket. Alba City? Mars? That was a red-eye flight. He'd have to call in to take time off. The Maxwell account was breathing down his neck. Ever since Kay ran out on him, she's been no help and he'd been swamped.

And yet, he had his tablet in his paws again, and soon he had sent off the warning. Luckily he had the day off tomorrow, but asking for a three-day weekend was bound to put some pressure on him. He'd have to make it up later.

Then again, what the hell am I doing!? He thought as he hit send on the message and stared at it with dread.

He felt helpless all of a sudden. Powerless. It had ended badly. It ended in the worst possible way. It ended with violence. When he woke up, he was this close to filing a restraining order or putting in a complaint to The Company with HR, but at the same time he stayed his hand. Any noise that Roy made would reflect back on him, and with Kay already spreading rumors about Sam, he needed to keep his reputation squeaky clean.

Regardless, he approached the rideshare, dropped his last cigarette on the ground and climbed in without a word. The driver, a chatty-looking parrot, turned around and said, "Early night?"

He stared at the parrot, and in a split second, made his decision.

"I need to head home," he said, hating himself as he typed the address into the console built into the back of the driver's seat, "And then keep the engine running. I've got a flight to catch."

Space travel wasn't cheap, but that's what expense accounts were for. As long as Sam managed to buy a box of staples or whatever for the office it didn't matter how far he went. Mars, he knew, had pretty lax imports, but even he couldn't get everything he wanted. He decided to frame this trip as research, trying to find a new distributor for good Martian potatoes – thank goodness for the foresight to look up Alba City before he climbed aboard the shuttle and got too far from a station's satellite reach to use the net.

He was dressed far more casually as he sat in the seat. Slacks, a light jacket, and the flannel button-down which he didn't bother to change out of. Instead of the chunky lesbian boots he wore for the club, he was back in his loafers. He didn't have anything to prove to Roy after all.

Roy. Sam didn't even bother interrogating why he was on a shuttle to go meet with Roy. It was simply no use. He didn't have an answer – at least not one to his own satisfaction – except that the man had an open invitation, and in-between the parts where Sam was scared for his fucking life, he sort of missed the times that they had together. It had been drifting into something... well, not healthy. Kinky, maybe, with how much Sam had enjoyed the power he had over the big bear and how much Roy clearly enjoyed Sam taking power. It was... pleasant. They fit together in an odd way. They fit in a way that Sam hadn't really fit with anyone before or since.

Inevitably, however, as Sam thought this, he would remember the pain of the bear's paw against his chin, sending him to the floor. He would remember the broken window. The broken mirror. The stalking. Roy was not a sad, lonely boy who needed love and tenderness to 'fix' him. He was not a romantic bad boy that Sam could turn into a project. He was a seriously disturbed man, and the rabbit had experienced that firsthand. So why?

Maybe because no one else will, he thought, before he scoffed out loud, *How very altruistic of you. Maybe you'll work a soup kitchen next.*

Maybe, he thought with a little sardonic smile, *You're just in the mood for a little danger. Maybe you're craving some more bad, rough sex. Maybe the thought of Roy's little episodes is making you harder than you care to admit to yourself.*

Maybe you should shut the fuck up.

He shook his head and leaned back before he reached into the carry-on bag at his feet and pulled out an eye mask, which he strapped over his eyes to keep the lights out of them. He then reclined his chair as much as it could, closed his eyes, and tried to get some sleep.

The trip went by faster than he would have thought. He slept through the red-eye hours, and even sort of enjoyed the feeling of absolute relaxation that traveling in Zero G gave him. That mitigated the stress of not being able to smoke for several hours at least somewhat. However, by the end, he was checking the time obsessively. Forty-five minutes to planetfall. Forty minutes. Thirty-seven. Thirty-four.

Eventually, he stuffed his tablet back in his pocket and then clutched his cigarette lighter like a totem. He still had to find Dublin Street and figure out which stretch of it number 36 sat on. Luckily Alba was one of the bigger cities on Mars, so he wouldn't have to shuttle into the city. He could just walk out of the space port, check a map, and start searching.

As soon as he stepped out of the airport terminal, the first thing he did was eagerly light up. At once, the mounting frustration that had been plaguing him through the latter half of the flight was lessened, and he gave a deep, breathy sigh. Only then did he look around.

Alba City was an eclectic mess of skyscrapers, low, flat industrial buildings, and long, grid-like roads built more for efficiency than style. One of the earliest terraformed cities, it was built under one of the Martian domes which cast the entire city in a haze of grey, filtered sunlight that made everything feel immediately cold, as if it was always mid-autumn or early spring. It was known as a center of business on Mars, which meant it was dour, industrial, and populous, scrubbed clean of any and all things that might be taken as dirty or disorderly. Walls were washed obsessively by repair drones, loitering laws were observed and enforced brutally, and all-in-all, Sam found himself missing the quiet grungy quirkiness of Seb Station, even if it was a stratified nightmare. At the very least, there the multigazillionaires could disappear into their private retreats and leave everyone else alone to wallow in peace.

Step one: find that damn address. Sam walked down the street away from the space port, staring down at his tablet in one hand while he held his cigarette in the other, occasionally taking a short drag. He typed the address into the tablet's search, and once he had connected to the Mars net, it was simple to track down. North Dublin Street wasn't very far, which made sense. Roy was a freighter, so living near the space port made sense, and the apartments near the port where constant shuttle landing and takeoff noises rattled your windows night and day probably drove down the rent.

He turned down a busy-looking street, and then up another, heading north, and soon encountered Dublin, a long stretch of squat-looking red brick tenements – red Mars clay bricks. Very chic everywhere else in the galaxy, but here it seemed like the cheapest building material available. He read the numbers on the apartment buildings. He was in the fourties and the buildings counted down by two the further south he traveled. Forty-two. Forty. Thirty-eight.

Finally, 36 North Dublin Street stood before him. Sam narrowed his eyes, looking up at the three story apartment building. It was obviously an old red brick rowhouse from early in the planet's history that the landlord cut up into apartments as the richest folks moved further away from the space port. A concrete stoop led up to the front door. The walls were cracking slightly and needed repair, and through the open windows, Sam could see laundry hung out to dry and the glow of television sets.

He walked up the stoop and was confronted by a locked front door and a panel with a menu of little buzzers. There were about half a dozen buttons, ranging from 1A to 5A, and then, at the bottom, Apartment B, with a little card next to it that said "R. Archer."

As soon as he saw that, Sam lost his nerve. His face fell and at once he ran back down the stoop and ducked into the alley beside the rowhouse before leaning against the wall to finish his cigarette and think. He had been moving on autopilot since getting on the shuttle to Mars, and now that he was here and Roy was just inside, he was suddenly terrified. He hadn't even texted to ask if Roy was home.

Sam wasn't one to get cold feet very often, but there in the alley, his hands shook as he finished his cigarette and dropped it on the ground to stamp out, before hugging himself around the arms. It was in that moment that he realized why he was really here.

He missed the bear. He missed Roy. He missed having someone around his own age that he could talk to. He missed being put on a pedestal and being almost worshiped and fawned over by a random guy who Sam picked up out of the gutter. His eyes went wide, and he knew one way or another he was going to contact Roy – if for no other reason than Sam couldn't afford to go stay at a hotel room on such short notice – and had to figure out what to say.

He pulled out his tablet and started composing a message. '**Hello**' seemed too formal, especially since he basically ghosted the guy after the punch. '**Im in town wanna fuck?**' seemed too forward, and didn't really address the discomfort between them. '**The hits just keep on coming** 🐰🍑' seemed tasteless.

Finally, with a frustrated groan, he decided to cut the bullshit. The words weren't coming, so there was a better way to do this. He reached down, unbuttoned and unzipped his fly, and pulled his underwear down, exposing his pink cock to the open air. In the alley, he was confident no one could see him as he pointed at it with his tablet's camera and snapped a picture.

Quickly stuffing himself back into his clothes with one paw, his other typed a caption.

> **Outside 🍆🍑 can I come in?**
> *Photo uploaded*

Almost as soon as he saw his cock on the message screen, he wondered if he should delete it before Roy saw and figure out some other message. Two months of silence followed by a sudden, random dick pic was probably not the best look, but to be honest, Sam didn't care much. Neither of them had seen one another in their best light. He almost wished that Roy *would* tell him to fuck off, or to cut that shit out; anything to give him some excuse to go back to the space port, find a flight back to Seb early, and go back to his fucking life.

A notification popped up, and Sam stared at it, elation and dread mounting as he read the single word answer Roy sent him.

Yah.

Sam swallowed, before he rushed around the corner and back towards the stoop, finally buttoning his fly. He reached up to fix the fur at the sides of his face and to smooth out his ears before he pressed the button next to 'R. Archer,' and heard a muffled buzz. A few moments later, a louder buzz sounded and the automatic door lock clicked. At once, Sam pushed his way inside, and started to look around for Apartment B.

He didn't have to search for long, as the door with B on it was on the ground floor, obviously leading down into the basement. Sam approached it and before he could lose his nerve, he knocked and stood up straight.

It took Roy a moment to answer the door, and when he did, Sam's nose wrinkled. He smelled him first, a heady musk of filth and stale sweat that followed the bear up the stairs. Sam liked Roy's smell normally, but even this was too much for him. Then he saw the bear himself, wearing that trashy stained undershirt, boxer shorts, and nothing else. His fur was standing on end and his beard was unkempt. Bags under the bear's eyes made it clear he wasn't sleeping well, and the slight sway in his step and the open beer can in his hand made it clear that he was coping with hitting Sam badly.

The rabbit almost smiled. Maybe the best revenge for that smack on the face would have been to just leave the bear to wallow in his own misery and filth, but Sam didn't waste all this time just to gloat. At once he pushed his way inside without saying a word, and the bear let him by.

"S-Sam?" asked Roy as if he hardly believed the rabbit was actually there.

The apartment was clearly once a storage basement, as one had to climb down a set of creaky wooden stairs to get there. Sam ignored the bear's reaction and climbed down, peering over the stairs to see what it was he was working with. The room was a disaster. Roy was collecting cans and food cartons in one corner, dirty clothes littered the floor, and he saw broken remains of some unidentifiable piece of furniture in another corner. There was a bathroom off to the side with the door hanging open, and in another corner was a bare mattress sitting on a boxspring, stained by beer and food.

"Oh, absolutely not," muttered Sam, as he finished walking down the stairs. "Eugh! How can you live like this, you slob?"

"Sam, what are you... what are you doing here?"

Sam didn't answer. Instead he turned towards the bear, gave a sniff, and grimaced.

"God, you smell. What the hell have you been doing?"

"I... I never thought... I..." muttered Roy, eyes widening as if he realized this wasn't a hallucination.

"You got a shower?"

"Y-Yes, but—"

"Well, fucking use it," Sam said, walking across the room and stepping around various debris until he got to the bathroom door and peered inside. It was filthy here as well, with yellowing porcelain on the toilet and shards of mirror in the sink. Sam looked up at the medicine cabinet, realizing that the door was missing, and he looked back at Roy with narrowed eyes. "You really live like this?"

"Sam, I... I want... I wanna say sorry," said Roy, charging forward. However, Sam raised a paw to stop him and raised his other paw to cover his nose.

"No. Absolutely not. Come on."

"Wha…?"

With that Sam entered the bathroom, thankful that there were at least no shards of glass on the floor, and approached the shower. He pulled back the clear plastic curtain and looked inside. There was mildew at the corners, and it was badly in need of fresh grout, but it was functional enough. There was even soap in a little dish built into the wall. Thank goodness for small miracles.

The rabbit began to take off his jacket as he turned towards Roy before hooking a thumb towards the shower.

"Strip," he said, "and get in. I'm going to clean up around here."

"Wha-? Why?"

"Because I am not going to be spending the night in a sty like this," said Sam, "It's disgusting in here."

Roy, slowly, stepped into the bathroom and Sam began to sidle around him. He was about to walk through the door when Roy pushed it shut and held it closed with one meaty paw.

Suddenly, Sam was trapped. He was pressed against the wall of the bathroom by Roy's presence, and as he looked up, he saw the sheer emotions in the bear's face.

"You came," muttered the bear, tears appearing at the corners of his eyes. "You actually…"

"Not yet, I haven't," said Sam with a smirk, trying to make jokes. "Are you going to let me out or…?"

"I want to say so many things to you."

"Uh huh?"

Sam's instincts were firing again. He looked around the room. No windows. The only way out was the door Roy was holding shut. There was a thrill of fear shooting through his stomach. He was getting hard.

"Okay," Sam said, carefully, "like what?"

"I… I missed you," said Roy, eyes hardening as the hand

holding the door curled into a fist.

"Cool."

"And..." he continued, "and... I shouldn't have... I shouldn't have tried to keep you all to myself. I want you back. I'm... I'm happy to... to do anything to..."

"Then let me out of this bathroom," said Sam, slowly, letting some of his worries sneak into his voice.

Roy glanced at the door then, before he glanced back at Sam and asked, "You're... You're not going to disappear again, are you? I... I want to... I want to..."

His other paw reached up slowly and made to caress Sam's soft fur. Sam shivered, pressing himself back against the wall with nowhere else to go.

"Not until you take a fucking shower," Sam said, trying to make himself sound in control, although he was sure the fear he was feeling cut through it. "You really do stink."

"Do you... Do you want to take it with me?"

The suggestion took Sam by surprise. He was relieved to see the bear's fist uncurl. He wished he knew what Roy was thinking in that moment, but at the same time, didn't he come here to do just this? Spend time with Roy? He swallowed and cleared his throat before he shrugged his shoulders.

"If it gets you to wash out your dick and ass, sure," said Sam. "Plus it was a... pretty long flight. I'm probably pretty sweaty too."

"Yeah."

Sam looked around, glancing at the mess of a bathroom. There was one towel on a rack, which he hoped was clean, and the mirror above the sink was shattered. Nothing to be done about that. Slowly, he reached up to start unbuttoning his shirt.

"Let me put my clothes on the bed or something," said Sam, "so... so they don't get wet. I only brought the one set of clothes."

"Oh."

"You don't have bedbugs or something, do you?"

"I don't think so."

"Better fucking not," said the rabbit, before he glanced at the door. The bear had not moved his arm. "So? Gonna let me out?"

The bear hesitated for a moment. Sam felt the bear's other paw caress down his neck, touching his collarbone and reaching down under the clothes he was in the process of unbuttoning. Fear shot through him. He really was at Roy's mercy here in this tiny room. He had to get out of here.

He was sure Roy was going to reach down and start getting grabby when the bear slowly stepped away from the door, sidling past as he started to pull his undershirt over his head. Taking that as his cue, Sam hurried out of the bathroom.

He was breathing hard. The combination of Roy's unwashed musk and the heat of their bodies in that unventilated room made him light-headed. As he stepped out of the bathroom, he glanced over at the stairs leading up to the door. He could make a run for it. Roy hadn't changed, it was clear. He was still obsessive as ever, and coming to visit had been the biggest mistake of Sam's life. He needed to run away right now while Roy was getting ready to shower. He needed to run out into the street, find safety, and get off this planet – hell maybe ask for a transfer off Seb Station! Even if it ended up being a worse assignment, anything was better than letting that bear know where he was.

Instead, he turned towards the boxspring and finished unbuttoning his jacket and shirt. He stripped them off and then unfastened his girdle before he kicked off his shoes, undid his fly, and started to step out of his pants.

He heard the sputtering of the shower starting up. He hesitated for only another moment as he hooked his thumbs under the waistband of his tight red briefs. With a grimace, he furrowed his brow and eventually, his dick won out over his sense. He peeled off his underwear, his compression socks, and, finally, fished the bottle of lube out of his jacket, just in case. They were well past condoms at this point, and Sam knew Roy was probably clean, and that's all that mattered to him.

He laid out his clothes on the bed to keep them clean – or at least clean enough – and stepped over the mess back towards the bathroom. When he opened the door again, he saw Roy standing, nude, hard cock in his hands as he slowly stroked himself, waiting for Sam before he stepped into the shower. As he glanced over, he saw his hand start stroking faster at the sight of the rabbit's own naked body and hard cock.

Sam pointedly placed the bottle of lube on top of the toilet's cistern where they could both reach it from the shower, and then walked past him into the grimy-looking tub. The water was warm and pleasant. One last shower.

Soon, he felt the fat body of the bear step in behind him, and he almost dreaded turning around to face the man. However, the choice was taken out of his hand as the thick paws of the bear took him roughly by the shoulders and spun him around. As water cascaded down Sam's black and white fur, Roy bent one thick arm around the rabbit's waist, pulling him into the bear's body hard as he bent down and once again forced the rabbit into a hard kiss.

This time, Sam did not fight back. Somehow he had resigned himself to this – to sex or death or whatever Roy wanted. But there was another part of him that was still charged with power. He was sweeping into this man's life unannounced, and once they were done here, it wasn't the end. He would force the man to clean up; straighten out his life.

Sam gasped as the bear started to push him up against one of the walls of the shower, and he shuddered at the cold feeling of grimy tile on his back. Roy continued to kiss him hard, and as he did, his paws roamed around the rabbit's slight frame. Each kiss was ground lost. Each tender touch was an admission of feelings that Sam wanted nothing to do with. After a while, Sam moaned into Roy's mouth, feeling the bear pressing nearly all his weight on him as they made out.

Everything was warm and wet, and steam rose up around them. A bar of soap found its way into Roy's hands and he started to lather it before rubbing all over Sam's body. The rabbit breathed hard, blinking fast as he felt those rough hands all over him, but he couldn't help himself.

"Fucking…" stammered Sam, snatching the soap away from him, "You're the one who needs a fucking cleaning."

Sam lathered his own hands, and soon his own soft paws were exploring Roy's body, rubbing the grime and stale sweat out from between his folds and out of his fur. Roy was breathing hard, tongue lolling out of his mouth as he felt Sam's hands on him. Soon, the rabbit managed to reach down, taking his cock in paw and stroking it, before going lower between his legs and beginning to soap him up between his ass cheeks.

"This belongs to me," whispered Sam, "I expect you to wash it out better than this, in case I want a taste."

"Y-Yes, Sam."

Despite his submissive tone, Roy's bulk and thick limbs were keeping Sam tightly controlled as he used his hands to rub down his most sensitive places. Roy gasped and growled, hugging the rabbit to his chest and belly, until the rabbit pulled his hands out from his undercarriage and reached above to run them over the hot water.

Roy didn't need to ask permission before he did the same thing for the rabbit. He eagerly reached down, using the soap and the shower as an excuse to grope the rabbit's hard length, and to stick his thick, slick finger deep into the rabbit's asshole.

It was clear what Roy wanted from how eagerly he probed the rabbit's entrance. Sam gasped, clenching his teeth, before he finally had the presence of mind to get Roy to slow down.

"L-Lube…" he grunted, "The soap kinda b-burns…"

Roy whined, his own needy cock throbbing as he frotted against Sam's, but he took the time to reach out of the shower and pick up the lube. He poured a bunch into his paws, and then reached down to grope his cock, the water from the shower beading on Roy's oiled up shaft. He then reached under Sam once again, and the rabbit managed to lift up a leg as he did, gasping as those insistent fingers probed inside once again.

"A-Ah… fuck…" muttered Sam. His mind was racing for something to say – for some other way to pretend to be in control while Roy did exactly what he liked with his body. He finally managed to say "Y-You… You better fuck me good."

Roy only answered with a grunt before he turned Sam around, pushing him up against the tiled wall and making him whimper in surprise. Then, that bear cock was pressed to his entrance, and Sam clenched his jaw.

"Ah…!" he squeaked as Roy penetrated him slowly. The rabbit had to give him credit, he was a quick learner. He pushed in slow, a bit at a time, and seemed to be trying to match his pushes to the rhythm of Sam's breathing. Sam slowed down his breath to control the pace indirectly, and Roy followed course. The lube, the warm water, and Roy's gentle thrusts meant there was hardly any pain at all as Sam started to moan and cry out from the pressure inside. His paws scrabbled on the wet wall for something to grab on to.

Then Roy curled an arm around the rabbit's chest. He cried out as he was suddenly lifted up off his feet. Vertigo took over, and he screamed as he felt himself falling, but only happened to land cushioned on Roy's pillowy belly, cock still in his ass. He felt water on his face and sputtered, and he looked around to see that Roy had sat down in the tub on his knees for better leverage.

Then Roy began to fuck him.

All illusion of control faded from Sam's brain. His face was inundated with warm shower water that made him cough and sputter. The arm around his chest traveled down, groping and grabbing at his dick and balls as the bear plowed into him, and Sam could feel the slap of the bear's balls against the back of his own. He reached up to grab on to Roy's arms – the only leverage he himself had in the situation – and hugged them to his chest as that dick pushed in and out in long, slow strokes which were gradually getting faster and faster.

Sam breathed, or at least tried. He turned his face away from the water and managed to catch a breath that didn't make him cough. In all honesty, the water was annoying.

"H-Hey. T-Turn... Turn off..." he tried to sputter, but the feeling of Roy's cock ramming into his prostate caused his vision to blur and his cock to spurt. He closed his eyes against the torrent of water from above and focused on the feel of that cock, of the pillowy body behind him, of the strong arms surrounding him, and imagined the face of the bear, mouth open and licking the back of his neck, eyes unfocused, nose and ears blushing, and utterly dazed by the hard fucking he was giving the rabbit he had grown obsessed with.

"F-Fucking... w-wa... water..." sputtered Sam, trying to reach for the faucet. However, Roy held him tight and he couldn't move except to clench and unclench his fingers, toes, and ass.

A loud bellow came from behind him then as Roy seemed to start cumming. He held Sam tighter, pushing forward until Sam was facing the bottom of the tub. His knees were on fire as he was held like a ragdoll in that awkward position, hanging slightly above the bottom of the tub, and he felt wet warmth inside. He blushed. He'd been careful for a long time, but to have someone actually fuck him bare like this made his cock brick up. The annoyance from the water had killed his boner somewhat, but Roy, screaming and roaring in his ear as his thrusts grew short and desperate, made Sam hard anew.

Then, it was over. Roy's thrusts slowed down. He loosened his grip around the rabbit's chest and let him sink down to the bottom of the tub, and immediately Sam went to his hands and knees, gasping for breath.

"F-fuck..." muttered Sam.

In response, a gentle hand ran across the rabbit's cheek, and he couldn't hold in a small sigh. The cock in his ass was softening, and slid out a moment later, and for a moment they just stayed that way, sitting in the tub while the shower flowed over them.

"R-Roy..." grunted Sam, "Fuck... Ow..."

"Did I hurt you?"

"No, just... can't... can't really get up from this position," muttered Sam, a little embarrassed. "The, uh, the knees don't really..."

"Oh! Sorry!"

With that, the bear's arms, considerably more gentle than before, picked up the older man by the shoulders and stood up with him, helping him back to his feet. Sam hissed as his knees and back complained, as well as his ass. He was once again pressed into Roy's body, and then he closed his eyes at the feeling.

They stayed like that for a while, idly showering, until they were satisfied. Sam was still half-hard, and Roy half-heartedly made movements to try to jack him off. Sam merely shook his head and continued the shower, and as the water went off and they took turns drying off with the one towel, they stared at one another. They had fucked before, yeah, but that seemed *different.*

"What about you...?" asked Roy after a moment, realizing that Sam hadn't cum yet.

Sam smirked, before he reached forward to take the man's hand and lead him out of the bathroom.

Sam groaned as he lay back on the mattress, using the towel to protect his raw ass from the bare mattress as Roy knelt on the floor, an awkward mouth full of rabbit cock. Sam was astonished to realize that Roy wasn't the worst blowjob he had ever gotten. His mouth was big, his tongue long, and he was eager to explore and willing to slather him all over, from balls to tip. He even ran his tongue under the rabbit's fuzzy taint not far from his newly fucked ass.

Sam himself took long, slow breaths as he enjoyed the feeling. Amateurish as it was, the situation had been enough to get him harder than he had been in a while without medical assistance, and Roy was taking full advantage of it. His huge paws roamed over Sam's body, up his chest, and over his legs, and Sam himself ran his own paws through the fur on Roy's head, gently guiding him to bob up and down.

"Yeah, fuck," groaned Sam, "that's it, cocksucker. Good job. Best fucking mouth I've had yet."

A lie, but hey! Every now and then, a little praise made all the nasty names worth it. He saw Roy redouble his efforts at this praise, and he even gripped Sam's body to control his movement and keep him seated while he pushed that cock closer and closer to the back of his throat.

"Yeah! Fuck, yeah!"

He thrust up, pushing more of his dick in, and he saw Roy's eyes narrow as the dick no doubt touched the back of his throat. He saw the bear gag for a moment and smiled. The bear continued regardless, and Sam's grin only grew. He was hungry for it. However, no matter how hungrily Roy sucked, Sam knew it wasn't going to last. With a sigh, he felt himself get softer.

Roy, desperate for things to continue, fondled the rabbit's balls and licked up the entire shaft. He looked up at Sam with worried eyes that nearly broke Sam's heart, trying to get the other man hard again.

"Am I...?" asked Roy, suddenly self-conscious as he used his paw to stroke the softening dick, "Did I do something wrong...?"

Sam narrowed his eyes. He considered stringing the bear along as revenge for that hard fucking in the bathroom, but eventually he shrugged his shoulders and gently reached down to push the bear's paw off his cock. It fell limp over his balls.

"Nah. I figured that would happen eventually," muttered Sam with some bitterness, "After all, you didn't really give me time to take my little blue pill."

"Oh," said Roy, staring at Sam's dick, which remained half-hard and twitching, but had lost a lot of its vigor.

"I just have trouble staying hard, but hey, it still felt pretty good," said Sam with a sigh, before he leaned back on the mattress. It was kind of low, and Sam knew his knees and back wouldn't like it much, but he would live. "You mind if I have a smoke?"

Roy shook his head.

"Cool," said Sam, reaching over to his jacket before pulling out his pack and lighter. He looked around the filthy room for a while, before grimacing. "You got an ashtray or something? Or should we just sweep them up when we clean this fucking sty."

"Oh!" said Roy, before he looked around. He soon found a solution, standing up and rushing over to a discarded beer can. He shook it around, before he poured the dregs down his throat, and then brought it to the rabbit. All the while, Sam grimaced and smiled at the sight of that fat, hairy body padding around, as well as those heavy balls of his swinging like a pendulum. Sam crossed one ankle over the other as Roy put the can down next to him, eager to please.

Sam glanced down at it, and then up at the bear, before he flicked his lighter on and took a deep drag. He sighed as the smoke gave him a lovely feeling of contentment and relaxation, before he tapped the first ashes into the can.

"Recycling. Cute," said Sam, words dripping with sarcasm. He was relaxed now, in a position of power. Roy was waiting on him, and Sam prepared himself for the next step. They would need to pick up at least the trash on the ground, maybe sweep, certainly do some laundry...

"Sam," said Roy as the rabbit considered his next words.

"Hm? What?" asked the rabbit, before he looked down at the pack on the bed and smiled, "You want one?"

"S-Sure... but... I..." he said, reaching over the rabbit to take a cigarette, which he held awkwardly, "but... I really wanted to... to ask you something."

"Uh huh?"

Used to the ritual and taking strength from it, the nude rabbit felt extremely sensual as he leaned over to offer the bear a light. It didn't matter that he had a pot-belly, swollen ankles, and a dick that barely worked without some chemical aid. In that moment, he was twenty again, lounging around post-coitus in some co-ed's dorm or even a horny bachelor's pad, making use of the things he always prided himself on – his body, his wit, and his style. His body might be going, his wit might be duller, but his style? Well, the flick of his wrist and the delicate way he leaned his face towards Roy's as he sucked in a lungful of smoke? That was well practiced and had the desired effect. The bear blushed like a virgin, eyes wide, as if he hadn't brutally fucked the rabbit less than twenty minutes ago.

They stared deep into one another's eyes, Roy looking confused and Sam confident. However, soon Roy leaned away. Of course; he'd gotten his rocks off. Post-nut clarity. Sam sighed as he leaned back on the bed and waited for Roy to finish.

"Go on."

"Why did you come here?" asked Roy, finally. "I hit you."

Ah. *The* question.

Sam cleared his throat then, using the cigarette in his paw to stall for an answer, before he managed to find something to say, "I was... bored."

"Bored?"

"The Seb Station docks weren't fun anymore," muttered Sam. "All the queer kids figured out I was just a dirty old man, everyone older than thirty already knows what a disaster I am, and even the curious fratboy market has dried up. I'm... not really welcome in that scene anymore. Hell, even the girls in the office are starting to talk ever since Kay told them all about... you showing up at my house."

"Oh."

"I still haven't forgiven you for that, by the way. My HOA was not pleased to have a shouting match on my lawn at one in the morning. They were this close to hitting me with a fine."

"S-Sorry..."

"You better be," muttered Sam, looking away and feeling just a touch of guilt as he saw the pain on Roy's face. He quickly went on, "Anyway, I guess... I was bored, and you were honestly the last time somebody was... interesting. And... interested."

"Really?" asked Roy, eyes widening. "I'm interesting?"

Sam ran a paw over his head, considering his words, before he said, "I mean... maybe not in a good way, necessarily. You did... y'know..."

He mimed a boxer's right hook while making a silent 'pow' with his mouth. Roy blushed anew, this time from shame.

"Look, I'm not an idiot, and I know you aren't either. I know what you're thinking: this is a bad idea," Sam said, his voice lower now that he was past the jokes. "You're a freighter I'll barely see most of the year, I'm the biggest jerk you've ever met. Since we met we've done nothing but hurt and belittle each other…"

"I mostly hurt you and you mostly belittle me," said Roy, his voice low but insistent.

"Oh, boy's got a spine all of a sudden," quipped Sam before he could catch himself, proving the bear right and cleared his throat. "Yeah. You're… You're right. But… well… you love me."

Roy's eyes widened further. His forgotten cigarette simply hung from his fingers over the beer can, hardly smoked, even though Sam was halfway through his.

"You love me," repeated Sam, his voice a little weaker this time before he straightened up and continued, "And the sex is getting better, though you did almost drown me in the shower."

"Do you…?" asked Roy, "Do you love…?"

"Don't go that far," muttered the rabbit, narrowing his eyes. "Everything I've said before still stands. I don't do relationships. I don't do love. But you… I'll… I'll do you for a while, sure."

"That makes no sense," said Roy. "You know what I want."

"I do," Sam answered, nodding, "and maybe that's another reason why I came. It feels pretty good to be wanted for once."

Roy stared at Sam then, unmoving, like a statue. The cigarette in his paw burned away slowly and the stream of smoke was thinning out as it burned without anyone sucking more air through it. Sam idly thought that was a waste of a good smoke but knew better than to bring it up right that moment.

"When I left you at the diner..." said Roy, speaking slowly, putting one word in front of the other as he spoke. It sounded rehearsed, as if he had said this many times to the air, and he said it with disbelief, likely believing he would never get the chance to say it to its intended audience. "When I left you, I... I thought I was going to die."

"Oh, well..."

Roy barreled on, knowing Sam could take back the conversation with one of those quips if he let him, "On the way to my next stop, I couldn't stop thinking about you. Thinking about... hitting you. Thinking about what I did to you, and... what you did to me."

"What *I* did...?"

"There's a tricky spot just beyond Jupiter's orbit. Lots of concentric orbits all piling up. Y'gotta make sure the navigation computer is on top of things and make sure you don't interfere with it, so it can guide you through. Otherwise, there's moons and satellites all over the place you can run into."

Sam was silent at this, frowning. He simply smoked his cigarette.

"Lots of hotshots? They like to try to switch over to manual and drive through that stretch without the nav. It's hard, but you can do it if you know the patterns. Do the math."

"Sounds... risky," muttered Sam, not liking where this was going.

Roy nodded, before he looked down at the cigarette in his paw and, remembering it was there, reached it up to his maw and took a long drag.

"It made me think that... when I was a kid, my grandma had this berry bush. Sweet raspberries, and every year there were tons and tons of them. The kind of thing you never forget the taste of, y'know? But the bushes were old and crept over her lawn a little bit more every year and she was getting old and didn't really have it in her to prune them back anymore.

"So... one year I... I went out without telling anybody. It wasn't picking time yet, but it was noisy inside. People were talking. Yelling. I decided I wanted to go out and pick by myself. So I did."

"Uh-huh? And what does this have to do with...?"

"Shut up," hissed Roy, the harshest words he'd ever served to Sam, which made the rabbit back down immediately. "I picked a bunch of berries and ate all of them. I didn't want to leave any for anyone else. Then, the section of bush I was picking from was getting bare, so I had to reach further and further into the berries inside the prickles. They scratched my arms, but... I kept eating and eating.

"Then, a thorn caught my shirt, and I panicked and screamed. I lost my balance and fell into the bush, and... and I was suddenly surrounded by darkness and thorns. I closed my eyes and screamed as... as it felt like that bush was stabbing me all over. I struggled and tried to climb out, but it was pulling my clothes and fur and tugging at my ears, and... and..."

Reliving the experience was affecting Roy as his wide eyes slid off Sam.

"I thought of that, looking at the tangle of satellites the nav was getting ready to guide me through, and... I wondered if it would have been better to just stay in the brambles. Lie there. Let my parents and grandma forget about me and just fight each other. I... I thought about switching the nav off."

"God... Roy..."

Roy was snapped out of the memory, like leaving a trance, and seemed to realize that Sam was still there. He blinked hard before he took another drag on the cigarette and tapped the ashes into the beer can.

"You're here now, though," muttered Roy, "And... you

want me."

"I... y-yes, well..." stammered Sam, unsure of how to feel after that story. His shoulders slumped slightly as he shook his head and dropped his cigarette butt into the beer can's mouth. "Why tell me that? Just to make me feel bad? It worked, I guess."

"N-No! No! I..." muttered Roy, before he paused, and then said, "I don't know. I just... I'm glad I'm, y'know, here."

Sam paused for a moment, before he narrowed his eyes. With horror mounting on his face, he muttered, "Did you do it?"

"Hm?"

"Turn off your nav?"

Roy paused, staring at Sam, before he said, "I'm here, aren't I? I didn't crash."

"I guess that depends how good your math is," Sam said, as he slowly stood to his feet, his knees complaining the whole way. "Ugh. Alright, enough sob stories. Next I'll be telling you how much I miss my kids, and I do not want to go there, no matter how much you love me."

"You already told me about them," said Roy, "Two kids. One hates your guts, the other your ex..."

"Aaaalright, wise-ass, get your ass up. If I'm going to stay here another minute, we are going to clean this shit up," Sam said sharply, as he turned and picked up his clothes. He started to dress, and as he did, he looked around and said, "You change into something clean – or at least clean enough. You got a washer and dryer in this dump?"

"No."

"Well, then I'll run your clothes down to a laundromat or something," said Sam as he started putting on his tight socks with a pained grunt, "And meanwhile you find a trash bag and anything that's in pieces, shards, or belongs in a trash can? Toss it. And fucking find a sheet to put on this bed. I am not sleeping on a bare mattress."

"You're... You're going to stay..." said Roy, eyes wide. He simply sat there, naked, stunned by the revelation until Sam turned and, to his delight, smiled wide.

"I guess so," he said, trying to make putting on his sock look like he was slipping on a seductive pair of stockings, despite how much effort it took to roll them up over his puffy ankle, "but only if you clean up, you got it?"

"Yes, Sam!" said Roy, who stood up at once before finding a pair of boxer shorts to slip on and getting to work. He found a roll of garbage bags in a cupboard and, with sprightly steps that Sam wasn't sure he had ever seen from the big bear before, he began picking up trash, starting with their impromptu ashtray.

Sam watched him for a moment before he turned back to his clothes. Pants, girdle, shirt, jacket, and finally shoes. He started to gather up whatever the man owned that looked like it was even sort of wearable and packed them into another garbage bag before he slung the bag over his shoulder like Santa Claus and started to walk towards the stairs leading up.

"Sam, wait!" cried Roy.

Sam turned, ready to ask what the hell the bear wanted, but he didn't get a chance. Before he could say anything, the bear had rushed forward and bent down to kiss him. The rabbit, in a split second, dropped the laundry to the floor, threw his arms around the bear's neck, and soon their muzzles were pressed against one another, mouths open, tongues dancing. Sam closed his eyes, melting into the kiss. He was full of feelings for this bear in that moment, and, not wanting to admit to anything he would regret, he decided to call that feeling 'pity' and pressed his mouth harder into Roy's.

They stood like that for what seemed like half an hour,

making only soft grunts and the wet smacking of their kiss. Their paws roamed around, and for a moment, Sam was sure Roy was already up for round two. He would be as well as soon as he finally took that pill. He would have to take the little blue pill around when he'd loaded the washer, and by the time he was back at Roy's place, he would be ready to give the bear his next lesson.

As he thought this, Roy was the first to pull away, looking at Sam with a look that was deeper than any look he'd gotten from anyone. His wife never looked at him like that. His kids never did. None of his other conquests ever showed him a look that was half as desperate or soft as the angle of the bear's eyebrows, and those wide eyes, and the little, tentative smile that formed at the corner of his muzzle.

In that moment, Sam knew he would never be able to get away from Roy. They were tangled up together too closely. The bear had gotten his way. Sam was staying. In two months when Roy was back on his route, they would meet again, fuck again, and part again, and if Sam didn't want to die, he would go along with it, and have some fun besides.

Maybe even… thought Sam with an evil smile as he reached up to run a paw through Roy's beard. He then pulled it hard, pulling the bear into another kiss, this one surprisingly tender, before he smiled and picked his laundry back up.

"See you in a little while," said Sam. "This place better be fucking spotless."

"Yes, Sam," said Roy, his voice quiet and brimming with excitement.

SEVENTH ENCOUNTER:
HOME COOKED MEAL

ROY grunted as he stared, eyes wide, at the brand new magazine he'd bought. He leaned back in his chair, huffing as a stacked wolf with hard, clenched abs stared back at him, arms up and behind his head. Eagerly, Roy let go of the magazine, letting it float in Zero G as he used his fingers to turn the page. The wolf was in bed with a panther. Helpful text explained who these two strangers were, but Roy was too far gone.

In still images over the next few pages, the wolf had his mouth around the panther's hard cock while the panther sneered down at him. Next, the panther was pulling the wolf's fur as he arched his back, howling, with a magic view of the panther's cock shoved into the wolf's ass. Then, the next page started all over again with a twinky looking lion, smiling and innocent on a beach, where a bear – *oh god* – a burly, muscled bear encountered the young lion and laid him down on the beach, and… and…

Roy cried out, leaning back against the seat of his freighter. He threw the magazine aside so none of his floating cum would spill over those precious pictures. He had gone through the magazine three times over the trip ever since he bought it back at Alba. Men. Men were beautiful. Roy felt freer than he ever was in his life at that moment. He was so blissed out, he almost missed the floating blobs of cum trying to make way to stain the ceiling.

Sebastian Station was coming up. Six hours or so. He was going to see Sam again. The thought of the rabbit's body was enough to put him right back in the mood, but he knew he had to refrain. He was going to see Sam. He had to be able to perform for him.

The difference between the last time he made his freight route and now was night and day. He found himself playing with his action figures more often, talking to himself, humming tunelessly, and staring through the viewscreen outside making up constellations: The Rabbit. The Aging Playboy. The Lonesome Trucker. Paws clasping Paws.

He found himself laughing at jokes he told himself, and even, occasionally, spent some time reading those articles between the pornography. Apparently the wolf and the panther were established porn stars, while the lion twink was a new up and comer, and the bear was an old dab hand. Roy found himself curious. There was a whole world that he had been denied. He had lived in the dark for so long, and now, he wanted to know more about that bear.

He checked his instruments as he stuffed his cock back into his jumpsuit and saw that he would be arriving in Sebastian Station in five and a half hours. He put his legs into the resistance bike pedals built into his seat, deciding that exercise might be a good way to make the time pass. As he did, however, he got out his tablet. He was close enough to Jupiter's net to send a text that should arrive before him, and after all, he wanted to give Sam some warning this time.

About 5 and a half hours to Seb. Where should we meet?

He put down his tablet and began to cycle, controlling his breathing as he worked his legs. His mind went blank as he tried to push down his excitement, but soon, his tablet made a noise.

My place

Roy's eyes widened and his legs came to a full stop. Sam's place? Did he mean his house? Unease bloomed in the man's chest at the memory of the altercation on his front lawn.

I thought he only brought women home to...

Are you sure?

He finished the message and waited for a response, eyes wide. No hotel? No bar? Just an evening in? Was that even allowed?

theres goulash

And then 💔dessert💔

Dont make me regret it

Roy stared at the text. He wasn't a hundred percent sure what goulash was, but if Sam was making it, it must be good. Sam had good taste in clothes and cigarettes and liquor. Why wouldn't he have good taste in food too? His mouth already watered – both from a home cooked meal and the promise of 'dessert' afterwards.

He continued cycling, harder than before, almost imagining that the pedaling was going to make the freighter move faster. He had a dinner date to attend, and his heart was soon pounding in his ears.

Roy felt awkward standing on the curb in his jumpsuit. It was a quarter past one by the time he managed to hop out of his freighter and into a shuttle to Sam's neighborhood. He hadn't bothered to shower or change his clothes, but now that he was standing in front of Sam's beautiful house in his beautiful neighborhood, he was afraid to take a step forward, lest his footsteps somehow cause the manicured lawn to brown and for the earth itself to crack and swallow him whole.

Even so, he had been invited. There was goulash in it for him – which he had looked up once he was closer to Jupiter's net – and he was ravenously hungry. He began to walk up the front walk, up to the steps to the porch, and, hesitantly, rapped his knuckles against the door.

He stood there for several moments, hoping he wasn't making a mistake. Last time had been so wonderful it was almost too good to be true, but it still wasn't perfect. Sam was still Sam. The rabbit inviting him to his house had been a pleasant surprise, but now that he was here, he suddenly got a strange feeling in the back of his mind.

It felt like a trap somehow. Like a bully, acting like someone's friend, to lure a kid into an embarrassing situation. Roy was painfully familiar with that trick, and Sam… Sam was a bully. That was easy to see. He was cruel. He was selfish. But at the same time, he and Roy had already been through a lot together, and at this point, even if it was a trap, it was one that Roy would have happily walked into anyway, all for just a touch of that rabbit's soft fur.

He heard a lock turn over and soon the door opened. Sam stood in the doorway wearing a cozy knit sweater, brown slacks, and fuzzy house slippers. In one paw he had a mug of something warm and steaming, and as he stepped away from the door, he smiled.

"Roy! Come on in!" he said, smiling, "shoes off."

Roy stepped into a little mudroom where a selection of shoes were set out on a set of shelves for Sam's perusal. Roy found that he recognized several of the pairs. He hurriedly began to pull his boots off to try to comply with the rules of the house he was trespassing in, and soon he was standing there in his thick socks, looking suddenly embarrassed to discover that a claw was poking through the toe of one of them. He looked down at the sock, and then up at Sam, who merely smiled warmly and gestured for Roy to follow.

As soon as he was past the mudroom, he emerged into a living room, with off-white carpet, beige couches surrounding a false fireplace built into the wall, and a staircase leading up above into further rooms. The walls were full of art and photographs – scenes from nature, paintings of abstract subjects, and smiling family portraits. However, he only saw two people in any of the photos. The first was Sam himself, with his black and white facial fur, and the other was a younger man who was pure white with more erect ears but who otherwise looked a lot like a younger Sam.

"I've got dinner nearly ready in the dining room," said Sam with a smile, before he lazily gestured to the house. "Like it? Certainly costs an arm and a leg."

"Beautiful."

Sam stopped then, giving Roy an odd look, before he laughed slightly and shrugged, "Better than the digs you had back at Alba, huh?"

"Much better. You live here?"

"Import-export. Lots of things need importing and exporting," said Sam as he led Roy through a side door and into a dining room. There was wood paneling on the walls, and hardwood floors – or at least it looked like hardwood. Real wood would be a rarity this far from anywhere planetside, and the sight of it made Roy pause. Sam stopped at this, noticing, before he gave another laugh.

"Sorry to say," he said, tapping a slipper on the floor, "vinyl. Same with the walls. Still, cozy. And the table's real."

He knocked on the large round table, which had an electric crockpot resting underneath a round placemat. It did sound like wood. It was a modest table, but this far out, it must have been expensive.

"How much does importing pay?" asked Roy as he walked up and felt the wood of the table. "We don't even have this much wood on Mars."

"Not that much, sorry to say. It's an heirloom. Family used to live Earthside," explained Sam as he walked around the table and pulled out one of the matching chairs, offering the place for Roy to sit. "One of the few things I managed to get away from my ex. She may have gotten the house, and the kids, and most of the money, and my dignity, but at least I got to keep grandmama's table."

He rapped once again on the table, making a satisfying knock. Wooden stuff in Roy's room had been pressed composite pulp. This was the real deal. Sam stepped away from the table, then, and gave a wink.

"Back in a flash. I'll get us some bowls."

And with that, Sam left the room. Roy was alone, suddenly realizing that there was a delicious smell to the air. It was coming from the crockpot in front of him. There was an unctuous, savory aroma, and as he stood to get a better look, he saw what looked like pasta noodles and a red sauce inside, with chunks of vegetables. It smelled peppery and spicy, and Roy's mouth began to water anew. Soon, however, Sam returned with a stack of bowls in one arm, silverware in the other...

And with another man.

Through the door to the kitchen came a young-looking bull about as tall as Roy. He was wearing a jean vest over a hoodie sweater, and loose-fitted jeans with holes in the knees. He had two mugs in his hands, a smile on his face, and was already mid-conversation with Sam, and by the way Sam was standing close and putting on his flirtatious face, the bull was a new mark.

"- just gotta serve it hot with bread and butter," said the bull, before he looked up and saw Roy, his face falling slightly at the sight of the fat freighter. "Oh. This, uh, must be Roy."

Roy stood up suddenly, eyes wide as he looked from Sam to the stranger, who approached, sheepish look on his face.

"Well, you're about what Sam told me!" said the bull with a friendly smile as he placed the two mugs down on the table, "Here, coffee."

"S-Sam?" asked Roy, before he gestured to the bull, "Who...?"

"Thomas here is on a solar system tour. Harvard boy, from Earth! I invited him here tonight."

"B-But I thought..." muttered Roy.

Thomas seemed confused at Roy's reaction and glanced over at Sam, looking annoyed, "You didn't tell him?"

Sam smiled and tilted his head, before he shook his hands dramatically and cried, "Surprise! 'Dessert.' For both of us."

Before Roy could ask anything else, Thomas laughed and picked up a bowl. He spooned a generous helping of steaming goulash into it, before offering it to Roy.

"Family recipe," he said.

Roy, however, was not looking at Thomas. He instead looked past him. The rabbit allowed himself to put on a little bit of a sensual smile to crack the domestic-looking exterior.

"I swear," said Thomas, who was himself starting to grow nervous that he had walked into something strange, "these hookups aren't usually so, uh, homey."

"Hookups?" asked Roy.

"I met Thomas here over an app. I figured it would be a, er, fun adventure. The fact the boy knows how to cook is a bonus!" said Sam as he picked up his own bowl and served himself.

Roy stared down at the bowl of goulash being offered to him. This wasn't how it was supposed to go. Who was Thomas? He didn't want anyone else here! He wanted Sam all to himself. He wanted an evening without any mind games. He felt his teeth start to clench.

"Roy," said Sam, before he ordered in a stern voice, "sit down."

The bear, before he could even understand what was going on, took the food and felt himself sit. He had no choice. This was his evening. He needed food, and he needed a place to sleep. He assured himself that it was still Sam here. It was just also someone else. He picked up a spoon and shoveled the hot goulash into his mouth, and the conversation began to pick up without him. It was background noise to him. He was too lost in panic to hear anything.

He thought it was settled. He thought this was going to be fun. Why...?

"How about you, Roy?" asked Thomas, friendly as ever.

"What?" asked Roy, harsher than he meant. Thomas' face fell, but Sam merely laughed.

"Roy's a little shy," he said, excusing the bear. "We were discussing planets we've visited. Thomas here is on a tour. Seb

Station is a stop on the way to a research station on Europa."

"We're gonna get a fantastic view of the Red Spot!" he said, sounding as if it was the second time he had said it. Roy gave another glance at the bull. The boy had filed his horns down and capped them with silver or steel – something shiny. Despite the ripped jeans and grungy look, Roy realized he was probably rich as well to be going to Harvard and to have enough left over to take a planet tour.

Thomas was rich and Sam was well-off enough to have a nice house and to have inherited a real Earth wood table. Roy was the odd man out here. He hardly had anything to his name.

"Live on Mars," he finally said. "Spend a couple months there a year. Spend the rest freighting."

"Where does your route take you, other than here?" asked Thomas, leaning forward in interest now that the bear had started speaking.

"Starts from Earth, though I don't get to go planetside. The dock is on the moon. Nothing much there," he muttered, stirring his goulash around, "then, pass by Mars. Get to go planetside there, though not in Alba, so… anyway, past Seb I go a little out past Jupiter's orbit to a midpoint station between Jupiter and Saturn, and then turn around and go all the way back. About two months to get from Earth to Seb, two months to get from Seb to the waystation and back."

"Damn, in that tiny cockpit?" asked Thomas.

"I've been in it. It's miniscule. I don't know how he does it," said Sam, gesturing with his spoon as if it was a cigarette. "Usually, Seb isn't even part of the route. Those asteroids bouncing around the belt have been profitable for me, considering the extra traffic through Seb Station. Pity they're about to get cleared off."

"They are?" asked Roy, "I… hadn't heard that."

"Oh, doesn't that mean your route isn't going to go through

this station anymore?" asked Thomas.

Both Sam and Roy fell silent at this, staring at one another with a sudden... what? Fear? Surprise? Relief? Neither of them knew what it was they were feeling, but neither could they tell what the other was feeling either.

"I admire that, y'know?" the bull said, smiling as he interrupted this meaningful look. "It's honest work. Money makes the orbits go 'round, as they say, and freight is huge business."

"Yeah..." Roy said, his voice low, before he took another bite and finally broke the stare between them, "good food."

"Family recipe!" said Thomas, "Happy to contribute. I heard there wasn't much good to eat on Seb Station, so when I realized I was going to have to spend the night..."

"Well, don't worry none, hon," said Sam, reaching over to place a gentle paw on the bull's arm, "you stay as long as you like, and after dinner, well..."

He winked, and Thomas blushed, before turning to stare at Roy. He seemed unsure of the bear for a moment, but still managed to smile. Dark thoughts ran through the bear's mind. Thomas thought he was ugly and was humoring him. Thomas is only going to want to fuck Sam and not Roy. Sam is only going to want to fuck Thomas and not Roy. Roy was going to be alone. Roy was going to be miserable. He was spiraling, until finally he scraped the bottom of the bowl.

"Want seconds?" asked Thomas.

"No."

"Well, then," said Sam, with a smirk, "maybe a little... dessert?"

"God, that's so cheesy," muttered Thomas, "But y'know it's kinda sweet."

"Sweet?"

"I dunno, getting your boyfriend a hookup as a present," said Thomas, smiling. "It's nice that you two trust each other like that. I'm down, and it's pretty hot."

"B-Boyfriend...?" said Roy, eyes wide.

Sam cleared his throat and stood, and all eyes turned to him before Roy could say anything. "Well, if you please, Roy, I think you should head up to the bathroom upstairs. It's the door just to your left once you get to the top of the stairs. I left *the stuff* there for you."

Another wink. Roy had no idea what that meant.

"O-Okay," said the bear, standing up, before he eagerly turned and walked away from the table.

Sam called after him, with a predatory lilt, "Thomas and I will keep each other company, but don't take too long!"

Roy found his way up the stairs pretty quick and rushed up them. The upstairs hallway wasn't too large – basically a straight hallway with white walls and pale tan doors set at even intervals. To his immediate left was the bathroom, and when he opened the door, he found an odd sight.

Sam had covered almost every surface of the bathroom with votive candles merrily burning away, and there on the counter surrounded by tiny flames were four things: two boxes of something that looked medicinal, an envelope with Roy's name on it, and a red rubber ball attached to leather straps. His eyes widened. Was that a gag?

Intimidated at once, he reached over the candles carefully and picked up the envelope first. Unfortunately, when he un-folded the card, he found that his eyes weren't up to reading by gentle candlelight, and so he had to ruin the effect by clicking on the light switch, bathing everything in pale fluorescent light. Suddenly it was a normal bathroom, with clean white tile and baby blue accents – tasteful and spotless, and so unlike Roy's.

He read the note and found that it was a list of instruc-tions:

Roy,

I'm yours, yes, and Thomas isn't going to touch me, but you're mine, too, and tonight I'm giving you away like a common whore. Strap in! You're bottoming tonight!

1. *Lose the clothes*
2. *Shower, you filthy fuck!*
3. *Douche (Do not get shit everywhere!)*
4. *Lube up for our guest*
5. *Put on the gag and meet us down the hall in the bedroom*

> *Sam*

Roy stared at the note and then at the boxes. Indeed, one was a fresh bottle of lube, still in its package, and the other was a discrete box with the word 'Enemeze: Douche and Enema Kit' on it. His eyes widened.

Was he really going to do this? He remembered, vaguely, that sometimes Sam would talk about this; passing Roy to someone else and letting them fuck him. When Sam had said it as empty dirty talk, Roy had gotten off on the idea, but now that he was in this situation, he felt a panic rise inside of him. He was going to have to perform for someone new. Today was supposed to be Roy and Sam's one day together. Bringing someone else into it, even someone who was nice and could cook like Thomas, felt wrong. Roy found that his skin was crawling. He didn't want Thomas to fuck him. He wanted Sam.

But Sam wanted him to do this.

Sam. Roy looked around at the nice house and the spotless bathroom, and all the *things* Sam had to his name. He knew about all of them, of course, but this was his first time being among them. He had an odd feeling then as he stood, holding the card limp at his side. He felt like one of the *things* that Sam had collected throughout his life: the nice shoes-off carpet, the Earth wood dining table, the polished bathroom tiles, the suits and windbreakers and shoes and shirts and red underwear... and him. Roy. A closeted freak who wandered into this situation blinded by the novel feeling of someone *wanting him*. Now he was here. He was taken. He was owned. Sam was finally claiming him, and Roy had the most uncanny feeling that once Sam was done with him, he would be crushed like an empty pack of cigarettes and tossed in the trash. That was what he wanted, wasn't it? This was what he was trying to accomplish, wasn't it?

Roy picked up the box of 'Enemeze' and stared at the picture. A squeeze bulb which was surrounded by little purple flowers. As he considered things, he heard footsteps on the stairs outside, and, in a panic, slammed the door shut. As he leaned up against the door, he heard Thomas and Sam talking, although he couldn't make out the words.

Was being handed over to Thomas like a borrowed cigarette really be so bad? Roy was hardening in his jumpsuit at the thought. The bull was young and pretty – he looked like the men in the magazine he'd bought. He should be excited, but something was bothering him. Something was nagging at the back of his mind.

What was he going to do? He wanted to leave. He wanted this to stop, but... he didn't know how to say no. He didn't know how to refuse. This was all so romantic. A nice home cooked meal, candles, perfumed douche... He should be flattered, but why then, did he feel filthier than ever? Why did he feel like somehow this was going to turn out badly?

Why, now that Roy had everything he wanted, did he feel nothing but dread and panic?

He heard a giggle, and a door slammed down the hall. They were waiting for him. Down the hall, they were waiting for him in the bedroom, where Thomas would fuck him. He imagined there would be rose petals and more candles. Sam's sheets would be shiny silk, and Thomas would be smoldering.

And he imagined Sam, smile on his face, showing off his buck teeth. A smile of pleasure, yes, but also one that was mocking him. A parody of romance. A faithful mockery of all the things Roy wished Sam would do for him, and all the things he wished he could do for Sam, all brought out in service to this kinky fucking fantasy.

Roy dropped the 'Enemeze' to the ground and turned around, opening the door and charging out. He rushed down the stairs, ran to the entrance, all but jumped into his boots as quickly as he could, and pushed his way out into the night. He ran out across Sam's lawn, eyes wide and teeth clenched, and looked around. He'd taken a rideshare here and didn't have time to call for another one to pick him up, but he knew the way to go. He started walking down the street, hurrying away from Sam's house. It would take him hours to walk the same distance a shuttle or a hover could bring him, but anything was better than what he had just left. Wasn't it?

"So, how'd you two meet?" asked Thomas, glass of wine in his hand as he lay on the bed.

Sam laughed, his own wine in hand as he lay back on the bed as well. He hadn't changed out of his sweater and khakis, even though Thomas had stripped down to a pair of blue boxer-briefs that framed his hardening package beautifully. The rabbit smiled. He was almost sorry he wasn't bottoming tonight, but today was for Roy.

"At the Waffle Station," he said, with the delivery of a punchline before taking a sip of wine.

"That diner where everyone fights each other?" said Thomas, cocking an eyebrow.

"Mmhm," said Sam, "It's kind of romantic, actually. I was on a date with another guy, and this asshole came up and started giving us guff for it, and then Roy stepped in like a goddamn wrestler and pulverized the guy with a chair."

Thomas laughed, covering his face with his hand. "Holy shit, really?"

"Yup!" said Sam, feeling an odd sense of pride remembering that, as well as the immediate aftermath. "I have to admit he wasn't my usual type, but, well, we, uh, hit it off. Seeing someone hit someone else over the head with a chair for you goes a long way. It's, uh, been kinda rocky. I was hoping tonight would be a fun way for us to get closer."

Thomas seemed a little confused at this and once again cocked a brow while taking a drink. Sam shrugged.

"I know, it's weird. Roy and I don't really... I mean, it's been a weird ride, let's just put it that way," explained Sam, before he smiled. "He likes it when I talk down to him; likes it when I use him. Humiliation and stuff. Y'know? We all have our kinks and turns out I'm kind of into it too."

"Heh, well, I'm happy to play the part," said Thomas, before he shrugged and put his glass on the side table before he leaned on his side facing Sam, supporting his head with one arm. "Honestly I was afraid he wasn't into it. He was acting weird at dinner."

"That's just Roy!" said Sam, putting down his own wine. It had been about an hour since they sent the bear into the shower. Surely he'd finished his business by now, "I can't say he's a sweetheart or anything – he's... physical when he wants to be, but he... well..."

The words 'he loves me' were on his lips, but he couldn't quite get them out. He realized he was feeling the urge to gush to this perfect stranger about the bear, and he furrowed his brow, reconsidering telling the guy anything. On the other hand, this is stuff he's had on his chest for months now, and it's not like he would ever see the bull again after tonight.

"He's not used to this. Being in a... relationship like this," said Sam, quietly, "and I didn't tell him you were coming. Hell, I was the one dragging my feet on admitting that there was something between us, and I... I wonder if I..."

Thomas looked up at the rabbit, confusion on his face as the rabbit fell quiet. Soon, Sam forced himself to smile and perk up. He wanted to see Roy. It had been too long. He turned to glance at the bedside clock and furrowed his brow. Over an hour. A tickle of fear in his stomach caused him to sit up.

"I'm going to go check on him," said Sam, standing up. "Don't get too drunk. I need your dick nice and hard."

"Nobody's ever complained yet!" cried Thomas with a wide bovine smile before he rolled over, snatched the bottle off the side table, and topped off his drink.

Sam turned then, walking down the hall towards the bathroom. He was suddenly deep in thought. He had a whole litany of things he wanted to say to Roy. He had been saving them until after sex, so nothing would get in the way – getting Roy to agree to something while fucking him didn't work so well last time, after all – but he wondered if he should have discussed them with the bear first. After all, it was a big change.

He approached the bathroom, but oddly, he did not hear the shower running, nor did he hear footsteps or Roy's usual grumbles as he muttered to himself. He narrowed his eyes, before he knocked.

"Roy, you almost done?" he asked, before he smirked and decided to play into the fantasy a little, "Tommy's waiting for his toy. He's getting impatient."

Silence greeted him. Sam narrowed his eyes. No reaction?

None? That wasn't like Roy at all. He knocked again.

"Roy? You alright?" he asked, panic sneaking into his voice. Roy was only forty-five, but he was still getting up there, and he was pretty fat. If there was something wrong... "I'm coming in."

He turned the doorknob and found it unlocked. He pushed his way inside and found that Roy had left the light on. Most of the candles had gone out, and in the little shrine Sam had left for him, the ball gag and lube were still sitting untouched, while the box with the douche in it and the night's instructions were lying on the floor. The air was cold. Roy hadn't showered. Roy hadn't done any of what Sam asked. The rabbit's eyes widened.

"Sam?" called Thomas from the bedroom, "what's up?"

Sam ignored him. His heart was pounding. Did Roy leave? Why? What reason did he have to leave? Was it Thomas? Did he get sick? He stepped away from the bathroom door, eyes wide.

"Sam?" Thomas called.

The rabbit ignored it, turning and running down the stairs like his life depended on it. He took the stairs so quickly that he felt his knees start to ache, and he grunted at the exertion but did not stop. He had done something wrong. He'd chased Roy away. Why? How?

Anger flashed in the rabbit's chest. *Why? How dare he?*

He left the house through the side door, snatching the keys to his hover off the little hook on the wall, and popped the door open before climbing inside. He turned the hover's ignition, and it began to float. Only then did Sam close the door and roll out of his driveway, before zooming down the road.

Where would he even go? Back to the docks? Maybe the shitty company apartments? They were planning this day for so long. Why would he...?

You were planning this day. You didn't tell him anything.

He leaned on the accelerator, entering the tunnel out of the suburbs quickly and starting to make his way back to the docks at the edge of the station. He only slowed down when the tunnel began to turn, making him grunt as it did. All the while, his heart continued to pound.

You had weeks to tell him. Weeks to ask him. You had so much time, but you were such a coward...

It took him maybe a half hour to get from the suburbs to the docks, a trip that usually took him an hour by shuttle. He didn't even think of his rules – never bring your own car. Never bring anyone to your house. Don't mix up your personal life with fucking around. None of that came to mind. The only thing he thought of was Roy.

You never thought of what you would do if he ever said no.

At two in the morning, it wasn't hard to find the bear. He was big, tall, and one of very few people on the streets this time of night. The bear was walking slowly, like a zombie, as he seemed to be walking back to the docks. With a sigh, Sam slowed down the hover, rolled down his window, and shouted.

"You son of a bitch!" he cried, making Roy jump and turn.

"Sam?"

"What the fuck are you doing, running out on me? I had everything set up!"

Roy stopped walking and Sam put on the brakes. They simply stared at one another for a while.

Finally, Roy, without a word, began to walk on.

"H-Hey!" cried Sam, matching the bear's pace in the hover, "I wasn't done talking to you! What the fuck is this?"

"I'm going to bed," muttered Roy.

"Wh-Why?" Sam demanded, "Goddammit, Roy, I thought... I thought we were past these fucking mindgames. I thought we..."

"I did too!" roared Roy suddenly, turning towards the hover and slapping it hard on the roof. Sam flinched at the loud noise and hit the brakes in surprise. Roy stared at him through the window, and for the first time Sam saw the bear's face clearly. He saw the tears streaming from his eyes. "I thought we were okay. I wanted to be with you."

"We were! Honestly!"

"A-Another trick," rumbled Roy, "a hookup, pawning me off on someone else…"

"It isn't like that! Fuck, Roy, I did this for you! Thomas is a present for you!"

"I don't want Thomas, I want…!"

Roy paused, frowning, before he turned and continued walking. Once again, with a grunt, Sam matched his pace in the hover.

"Can't we fucking talk about this?"

Roy shot Sam an angry glare. Sam matched it, but soon sighed deeply.

"I want to talk about it. Really. Forget Tommy, he was too nice to expose to our damage anyway. Forget the kinky little game. Get in the car."

Roy simply kept glaring, pinning Sam to the spot. However, Sam did not back down.

"Please?" asked Sam, his voice tender. More tender than Roy had ever noticed before. That stopped him in his tracks.

"No more games?" asked Roy.

"Scout's honor," said Sam, holding up a paw. "Nothing. I just… I just want to talk."

Roy was quiet for only another moment, before he nodded and started to walk around the hover to open the passenger side door. He climbed inside, ducking his head, and soon Sam and Roy sat side to side, staring ahead.

Sam started speeding up to the speed limit, and simply drove with no destination in mind. Both were quiet for a moment, before Sam cleared his throat.

"I'd say we could go get waffles, but we filled up on gou-lash," the rabbit said with a laugh, trying to fill the silence.

"You scared me…" Roy answered.

Sam glanced over then and saw Roy's face was pointed down at his lap. The bear seemed numb and was probably exhausted from the long walk. Even though the docks and Sam's neigh-borhood weren't that far from one another, walking through the space station's winding back corridors was probably a long, tiring ordeal, and not nearly as straightforward as using a hover or catching a shuttle or rideshare. Seb Station wasn't built for pedestrian traffic outside of its proscribed boroughs.

"I didn't mean to. That time," muttered Sam.

"You've scared me before. I… I was afraid… afraid I might do something to you."

"What? Hit me again? We're past that, aren't we?"

Roy did not answer.

Sam, desperate to keep the conversation going, breathed out hard, and turned down a road. He knew a spot along the docks – a cul-de-sac surrounded by warehouses that few peo-ple knew about. Drive down the alley between the warehouses, and one would eventually find their way to an empty lot which had a view of the dock's loading area below. Make-out point. It wasn't much of a view – basically scaffolds, catwalks, docked vehicles, and flashing lights – but it was something, and it was the quietest place Sam could take Roy.

As he cut the power to the hover and it settled onto the magnetic pavement, he stared out the front window, leaning against the steering column. Roy continued his silence. Sam knew that it would be up to him to explain.

"I know you liked me talking shit to you," he muttered, "You like getting humiliated and used and stuff, right? So I figured I'd surprise you. Y'know, like I've talked about before.

Kinda… get someone else to fuck you, tease you while he does it. I was going to spit in your mouth, and call you a bitch, and the whole nine yards. I thought you'd love it."

Roy's silence continued.

"I thought you were into that shit!"

"I… I guess I am," muttered Roy, scratching his head, "When it's with you."

"It was with me! I was going to be there the whole time, I promise!" Sam argued, frowning as he found himself starting to get angry, "Hell, if you'd just trust me…"

"Trust…?" Roy muttered, "I don't trust you."

"What?"

"After everything," Roy said, "why would I trust you?"

"But…!"

"Something always happens," said Roy, "I… I was afraid."

"That's not fucking fair!" cried Sam. "You're no fucking saint either. You're talking about shit I did when you're the one who fucking stalked me! Hit me! Hell, that time I visited, you were ready to basically rape me in the shower."

Roy flinched, listening to Sam go off. He thought back to then. Had he? Was that…?

Sam pounded on the steering column, frustrated, before he groaned and leaned forward. "What are we supposed to do with this, Roy? If it's not one thing, it's another. I didn't want this to be serious and you made it serious. Now I'm finally happy to play along, and now you're pulling back?"

"I'm… scared."

"Of fucking what?" demanded Sam, straightening up. Roy was astonished to see the rabbit's muzzle quivering a little, and he watched his eyes squint just a little more. He was holding back his emotions. "Every other time was worse than this. We were either at each other's throats, or we weren't ready, or something was just… off, or wrong, or painful. This time was fine. We were both safe. Forget Thomas, I can kick him out. It'll just be us. What's so scary about that?"

"I... I..."

"I was going to ask you to move in with me tonight," Sam blurted out then, and as soon as it left his muzzle, he regretted it.

Roy turned to stare at him, eyes wide.

"What?"

"I... I just..." stammered Sam before he reached up and swiped at his eyes, "this is a fucking disaster."

"You wanted me to...?"

"I was going to suggest you... quit your job. Live with me for a while. Maybe... Maybe find some work on Seb. I'd put in a good word at a warehouse on the docks. Get you out of that freighter."

"I... I need this job, Sam. I need..."

"I have money. I'm well-off, and after the HOA gave me shit, I figured fuck it," muttered Sam, "I... I dunno why I thought this would be a good idea."

Roy was quiet at this, eyes wide as he took in Sam's words.

"I wasn't afraid of the hookup, not really," muttered Roy, finally, "but... something felt different. Like you were... were finally settling for me. Keeping me. I thought I wanted it but... but I got scared. Scared that I'd be trapped there – like, you were giving me everything I wanted to lure me in..."

"And why not? I'm... I'm fifty-six, Roy. My dick barely works, my body is getting weirder every day, my knees hurt, and a... half dozen other things I don't wanna get into now. I have to lie to get any action anymore, and it's... it's never as good as I think it's going to be. But then you come along and... and..." He growled, running paw through his fur. "You never... you never cared. You saw me naked and didn't run screaming. I didn't have to pretend to be nice or polite around you. You... You looked at me, an over the hill fucking asshole and you said... 'y-yeah, that's fine.'"

His paw snapped to his eyes, covering them. He rubbed them, as if he had a headache, but by the loud sniff, Roy could tell he was on the verge of tears. He breathed hard, shaking his head and growled again, fighting against the oncoming tears.

"And... And I didn't see it. I just looked at you and saw a fat piece of shit I could take advantage of for a... a good time. It was a bad idea. I knew it, since that first time we met, and still..."

"You don't have to explain."

"I do, goddamn it!" cried Sam, a whine sneaking into his voice, "I... I scared you. Fine. I'm... I'm sorry. I should have talked about it before pulling that shit on you. I should have asked you to move in weeks ago. I should have told you... G-God, I want a cigarette so f-ucking bad."

Roy stared at the rabbit as he began to break down. He blinked his eyes. This wasn't like him. The bear realized something was different. He thought about the day's events. He'd been so worried about Thomas and the weird sex game, that he almost didn't notice the weirdest thing.

"Why not have a cigarette?" Roy said, slowly.

Sam paused, pulling his hands away from his face and looking up resolutely. He breathed in deep and ragged.

"I... had to quit," he muttered.

"Oh."

"They found a..." he muttered, gesturing towards his chest, "Damndest thing, it... it didn't push up against my lung at all, so I wasn't coughing or anything. Just... grew in and it started spreading outside the lungs and..."

"Oh..."

"I didn't even go in for a fucking cancer screening! I just had my yearly, and they took some bloodwork to make sure

I could still get a script for those fucking boner pills and... well... they called me in for another test and one thing led to another and... and they didn't even refill my fucking pills either! Thomas was going to help me because I..."

Roy looked away, towards the view of the docks from above. Sam fell silent as well, frowning deeply as he crossed his arms. Now that it was out in the open, he seemed to have calmed down slightly, only sniffing a little. The inside of the car was deathly calm.

"I haven't told anyone else," whispered Sam. "Not my kids. Not my ex. Just you. I didn't even want to tell you until... until I started on chemo. I thought maybe if you were living with me..."

"You really did want to trap me."

Sam snapped his head to stare at Roy, opening his mouth to argue. However, his muzzle closed, and he clenched his jaw.

"I'm scared, Roy. I don't have anyone else. I... I pushed everyone else in my life away."

"What about your sons?"

"The one who still likes me lives on Earth. It takes money to get here from there flying commercial, and the routes are still fucked up from the collision in the asteroid belt," he muttered, "I... I can't travel like this and by the time he gets here I could be..."

"I... I don't know, Sam," said Roy, his paws shaking, "you were trying to lure me in so you could make me... make me need you like you need me now."

"You do need me, don't you?" asked Sam, his voice seeming to skip past hope and settling on fear. "You love me."

"Do you love me?"

There was silence then, as Sam stared hard into Roy's face. He clenched his jaw, unsure of how to answer. Slowly, the rabbit looked down at the steering column in front of him and gave a deep, tired sigh.

"It's... complicated."

"Not for me."

"You're a nicer person than I am, Roy," said Sam, his voice low. "Believe me. Even with all the smacking me around, I know I'm bad news. I know it. I knew it even before my wife left me, and now, finally, it caught up to me. I... I have no one else, Roy. You're all I have. I don't know if that counts as love."

"That's the most pathetic thing I've ever heard."

Hearing his own words thrown back at him, Sam could only laugh, reaching his paws up once again to chase the tears from his eyes as he smiled. He finally breathed in deeply and then out, leaning back in the car seat. Together Sam and Roy stared out over the docks, saying nothing, doing nothing, and just considering their next words. The words that would dictate the rest of their lives.

"You know what would be hot?" said Sam.

"What?"

"If you strangled me to death," muttered Sam, "No more aching knees. No more swollen ankles. No more cancer. Just... you, finally getting exactly what you always wanted."

"I... I don't want... I don't want you to die."

"You sure?" said Sam, deathly calm now, "You want me, don't you? So, take me. All of me. Every last drop."

"You wouldn't be that selfless," muttered Roy, "Even if I... if I did... you'd find some way to keep me awake at night."

"I've thought you were going to do it, a couple times," said Sam, quietly, "and... I'm so fucked up I kinda got off on it."

"S-Still... No," Roy said, his voice harsh, but with a crack to it. His eyes were widening.

"I know," said Sam, with a sigh, "Not yet anyway. Doc says it's early enough that chemo might do the trick but... I'm gon-na be all fucked up in the meantime, and... and... there's a chance it won't work. I need… someone. Someone who can… help me."

"Oh…"

"Stay with me, or… or stop the pain if it gets to be too much," Sam said, his voice more even now. "I want to ask you one more time. Will you move in with me? We won't… We won't get another chance after this. Your route won't go through Seb after today."

"Yeah."

"So? I could… I mean…" he stammered, "I don't know if I'm even… I…"

He turned, brow furrowed, as he stared once again at Roy. Finally, as if taking courage from the bear's presence, he reached over and snatched up one of his meaty paws. He frowned, but only at himself, as he forced the words out of his muzzle.

"I… do. I love you."

Roy stared at the rabbit for a long time. He squeezed the white-furred paw in his own. Was it real? Could he trust Sam's words? He could have said it any time before now, but he didn't. He only said it now, after he needed something out of Roy. Was Sam telling the truth? It was impossible to know.

As Roy saw it, there were three choices. Leave and never see Sam again, stay and suffer along with Sam as he wasted away on chemo – maybe recovering and maybe not – or…

Roy turned to stare out the window again. It would take them a long time to find the body, and by the time they did, Roy's route would have changed. He would never see Seb Station again. They were alone. They tortured one another so much in the past several months. They made one another worse people, Roy understood that. He should hate Sam. He did hate Sam a little, deep down. He should have been eager to take this chance. Sam was vulnerable. The rabbit wanted it, as a mercy. Both would be free and would have gotten everything they could have ever wanted from the other.

And then what? Go back to freighting? Go back to his tiny prison with his wrestling figurines and his porn? Go back to torturing himself, instead of letting Sam torture him? Find some other sad, angry little man to become obsessed with, to start everything all over again? No. He couldn't. It was all too painful.

Maybe instead, he would put his foot on the gas of the hover and launch into the abyss himself. Then there would be nothing. An end to both of them in one fell swoop.

He looked once again at the choices, and only one of them gave him what he wanted. Only one choice gave him hope.

Roy didn't answer with words. He turned, leaned over the seat and, silently, pressed a kiss into Sam's muzzle. He reached up, running his hand along the rabbit's chest and neck, feeling him all over. Sam went limp, realizing that the choice had been made for him. Roy knew that Sam had accepted whatever Roy decided for him – whether that be an easy death or a difficult life.

Roy pulled his muzzle away and Sam whispered, "Fuck…"

Suddenly, the rabbit retaliated, shoving his own muzzle against Roy's, returning his kiss tenfold. His kiss was desperate and long, and he gasped between breaths as he begged with his lips for Roy to do… something. Anything. One paw roamed around Roy's soft body, pulling him in closer, while his other paw reached down and pulled on the seat recliner, suddenly making the rabbit fall backwards until he was almost completely lying down. Roy obliged, leaning all the way over to awkwardly press down on Sam with his body.

"R-Roy…" said Sam, his arms around Roy's neck.

For a moment, Roy's paws tightened around Sam's thin, veiny neck, and Sam tensed up, pressing closer, eyes growing wider. Sam couldn't breathe. He opened his mouth, as if to ask for one last kiss, desperate to taste his lover for the last time before he submitted himself fully to the bear. He felt claws digging into the soft skin of his neck, and the bear leaned his face in close to Sam's, hovering his face over the rabbit's mouth, where no breath could enter or escape. Roy's eyes, wide and wild, met the rabbit's, causing a rush of fear through his chest and stomach, but also causing his limp cock to twitch.

However, a moment later, he breathed in. The squeeze became a caress, and the caress traveled down his chest, feeling the desperate rise and fall of Sam's sudden breath. Roy reached down to recline his own seat then, and soon the two of them lay, side by side. Roy's eyes lost their wild-eyed malice as they softened into one of concern – fear. He was still afraid. Sam knew the bear's mind was also racing with thoughts of the future.

Sam breathed hard for a while, staring at Roy as the rest of his life lay out before him. He knew, then, what was going to happen. Every excruciating detail, watching his body grow even thinner, watching his fur fall out, feeling like death warmed over. He knew what was going to happen to him. He hadn't been prepared to face it alone. Now, he didn't have to, for better or for worse.

They were both trapped, now.

Then, Sam's tablet gave a small beep, and he furrowed his brow. He reached down to pull it from his pocket and stared at it with annoyance. However, it soon settled into a look of surprise, and then a sly smile.

Did you find him? 🐮 Is everything OK?

"I was right, that kid is too nice for his own good," Sam whispered with a smirk, reaching over to take the big bear's paw in his own once again as they lay side by side, "We could go home and let Thomas fuck you for me, or maybe the other way around if you're in the mood. Your night, your choice, big guy."

Roy met Sam's gaze then, considering it, before he squeezed the rabbit's paw and slowly managed a tentative smile.